BOOM TOWN

Also by Trevor Scott

BOOM
TOWN

Trevor Scott

Broadhead Books

Beaverton, Oregon

BOOM TOWN

Copyright © 2006 by Trevor Scott

Broadhead Books
P.O. Box 7396
Beaverton, OR 97007

Visit the author online at www.trevorscott.com

Library of Congress Control Number: 2006923770

ISBN: 1-930486-62-6

Printed in U.S.A.
First Edition

For mom

Acknowledgments

Thanks to the people of Bend, Oregon, the setting of this work of fiction. Having lived in Bend for more than nine years, I saw firsthand the development of a tourist town from a high desert lumber-based community. Growth is inevitable, but expansion without restraint can be irresponsible. I hope the housing costs never reach a level where the builder of those houses cannot live within the city limits. Bend is a great town, *Boom Town* or not, and I hope to live there again soon. Forgive me for placing streets and housing developments where they do not exist.

PROLOGUE

Leaning alongside an enormous Pozzi window on the second floor of his expansive house, Dan Humphrey stared wistfully at the darkness of the golf course below. A constant wind swept across the greens, bringing goose bumps to his naked body. Somewhere out there he could hear sprinklers swish-swishing—one last attempt to keep the championship course green before the snows of December swooped down out of the Cascades of Central Oregon.

Dan glanced over his shoulder dispassionately at the action on his king-sized bed. The new guy was on top of his wife pumping her with great ferocity, their bodies clashing in perfect harmony to an Enya song, as if the two of them had done it together hundreds of times, and his wife enjoying herself perhaps too much, Dan thought. As so many times in the past, Dan suspected he should be excited by now. Maybe reached his own goal. But, as he glanced down, he was as flaccid as a night crawler in a heavy rain. And all he could think about was his business. Could he walk away from his baby? That was the question of the week for him. And he knew deep down that his incertitude invariably led to sexual encounters that had become increasingly destructive. Yet, he also knew that he could not stop, could not go back.

He turned back to view his back yard and thought he saw something move along the edge of the grass among the sagebrush and small junipers. Probably a deer. They had eaten most of the flowers the gardener had planted.

His eyes focused on the hot tub on the flagstone patio below, thinking about all of the naked bodies that had soaked in there. He felt for any sign of life. Nothing. How had things come to this?

Letting out a series of panting, guttural sounds, his wife finally released herself and then crashed back onto the bed. Dan could see the reflection of the man come out of her, and then go directly to the bathroom. Through the corner of his eye he saw another flash of movement below in his yard. What the hell was that?

"What are you doing?" his wife asked him.

Dan turned to her.

She was on her side, her perfect naked body sliding against the satin sheets seductively.

Before Dan could answer, the man came back from the bathroom, his manhood still partially active after pulling off the spent rubber and wiping himself down. "Hot tub time?" he asked.

When neither answered, the man shrugged and left toward the staircase.

"You aren't jealous are you?" she asked, her tone hopeful.

"No."

"He was the biggest. Does that bother you?"

"I said no! Let's go." Dan headed toward the door.

She slowly went out after him.

Downstairs, a small, dim light shone from the kitchen and allowed the two of them to see their familiar surroundings. At the bottom of the stairs, Dan stopped and his wife came up behind him, her bare breasts pressed hard against his back.

A noise to his left. His eyes shot to the right, where the man was outside, his face illuminated by the hot tub lights. What made the noise? They didn't own a cat or dog.

Dan stepped lightly toward the living room, around the mission end table and the leather sofa, and then he stopped suddenly and his wife crashed into him.

"What's wrong?" she asked him.

Dan reached to her, grasped her hand and squeezed tightly, his eyes focused on the far side of the living room.

"Who's there!" Dan yelled.

"You're scaring me," she said, her breathing uncontrollably loud.

Suddenly, a flash and a bang. Dan's first indication that something was truly wrong was his wife's hand going limp in his, her body crashing to the carpet at his feet. There was no time for Dan to move. No time to react in any way. When the next flash came, it registered for a microsecond in Dan's brain before he seemed to float to the carpet and land at his wife's side.

CHAPTER 1

S tanding on a precipice over a hundred feet above the ocean, Tony Caruso folded his arms against his chest and took in a deep breath of sea air. Along Oregon's Cape Perpetua, there was always a strong breeze, cold and damp, the smell of wet death wafting up from the depths of kelp beds and volcanic tide pools. Sitting to his right, his Giant Schnauzer frantically wiggled its cropped tail against the low grass.

Tony thought back on the night he bobbed in the dark, frigid sea to the south, the silence unbearable and incomprehensible. His two fellow sailors had died instantly in the blast, he knew. That's the only way his mind could think. He would have died with them if fate hadn't intervened, having him step out onto the catwalk only moments before the bomb exploded. His ordnance partner had known the dangers involved with de-arming a thousand pound bomb, but the sea-going tug captain, a victim of a tragic accidental bombing by his own Navy, had only known that his vessel was listing badly and could sink in those dark, heavy seas. A part of Tony knew he should have been there with his friend; the other part, his logical, reasoning intellect, rationalized his existence as an inevitability of some higher purpose that he hadn't yet come to understand. Maybe more time would settle that for him.

His dog whined, turned its head, and then nudged its wet nose against Tony's leg.

"Hey, Squid," said a voice from behind him.

Turning around, Tony nodded at his old friend, Captain Joe Pellagreno, United States Navy Retired.

"What's up, Joe?"

Tony had been staying down the road in a condo near Yachets, trying his best to stay in wine and still find time to locate a missing sixteen-year-old girl, who had been trying her best to entertain the pleasures of a twenty-year-old commercial fisherman in Waldport when Tony found them together. His old Navy buddy had caught up with Tony squeezing the last drop of red wine from the box the night before, and asked to see him this morning when his comprehension would be more complete. Joe's disappointment had been painfully evident to Tony.

Joe Pellagreno hadn't changed much since his Navy days. He had always been a little thick about the middle, even though he ran three miles a day, and his hair, although a bit longer now, had only grayed slightly from the last time Tony had seen him in Seattle two years ago.

"What are you doing, Tony?" Joe asked, his sad eyes focused on the ocean.

"I've been hiking here every day for the past two weeks."

"You know what the hell I'm talkin' about. You've been drinking worse than a sailor."

Tony glanced at his friend. "You should talk."

"Been sober for a year."

"Great. Is that why you called me? To redeem me?"

Joe shook his head. "No. I heard you retired a year ago and damn near dropped off the face of the Earth. Brad Colby said you left under...for personal reasons."

Tony turned to his friend and grabbed his arm. "It had nothing to do with the explosion. I'm over that. Over twenty years in the Navy was enough."

"Listen. You were nearly killed. You lost your best friend. You lost your hearing in one ear. It's understandable you'd still harbor some ill feelings."

Ill feelings? If it were only that easy, Tony thought. He questioned daily if he could have done something more that night. Anything to save his friend and the captain of that tug. The Navy had given Tony a couple of medals for that screw up. Two men died and he got medals. Brilliant. A few more accidents like that and he would have been the most highly decorated sailor in the Navy.

"Joe, I can't lie about it," Tony said pensively. "I should have died with Johnny that night."

"You survived. You're alive!"

"I don't feel alive, Joe. I feel like I'm dying every day, little by little."

Joe let out a deep sigh. "Can you do me a couple of favors, Tony?"

If there was anyone Tony owed a favor, it was Joe Pellagreno. When the Navy had tried to give up the search for him in the ocean that night, Joe had stood his ground, making them look longer, knowing Tony was alive.

"Name it."

"I retired to Bend. Have you been there?"

Tony shook his head.

"It's a great little town," Joe said. "A good friend of mine owns a gallery there. I showed her some of your photos and she wants you to show them just before Christmas."

Tony shrugged. "I don't show my photos."

"They're beautiful, though. You've gotta show them, Tony. She's especially interested in the faces series."

She had good taste, Tony thought. Those were his favorites also. He had taken a series of stark photos of weathered faces in his travels around the world. But to show them? He wasn't sure about that.

"You think it's a good idea?" Tony asked.

"Yeah, I do."

"You said a couple favors."

His old friend shuffled his feet and then turned his head to

Tony. "Another friend could use your help. His son and daughter-in-law died and he suspects there's more to it than the police are saying."

"A double murder?"

"Maybe. That's what we want you to find out."

Since Tony's retirement from the Navy a year ago, he had helped out on a few arson and bomb investigations in the Pacific Northwest, working as a consultant for the Portland and Seattle police. Six months ago he had picked up a private investigator's license from the state of Oregon, one of the easiest to obtain in the country, and started his own company. Although Tony had helped on some murder cases for the police, those had always dealt with an explosion of some type—his specialty.

"I'm not really qualified for that," Tony said.

Joe hesitated and finally said, "Well, they say this guy's kid shot his wife and then blew up his house."

"The murder suicide I heard about in the news?"

"That's what they're calling it," Joe said. "But there could be more to it. Tony, could you just go over there and look into it? It could be just what the police say. Then you do your gallery showing, sell a few photos, and make a few bucks off the investigation."

Having heard about the incident on the Portland news in his condo, Tony wasn't sure he wanted anything to do with it. The father had been denying his son could have done it. And he was a powerful real estate developer in the state.

"You got room for me in that condo?" Tony finally said.

"I won't be there. Ute wants to go to Switzerland for a couple of months. Her family owns a chalet in Grindelwald."

"Must be nice."

"They've already got a shitload of snow." Joe's eyes sunk toward the ground, and he added, "You can stay in my condo until I get back in late January."

Tony thought about it. He didn't currently have a home. Since a few months back when he became his version of the wandering private investigator, he had not figured out where his home base would be. Maybe he didn't want anything permanent. He would never move back to Duluth or anywhere near Minnesota, that was a fact, but beyond that, only time would tell. Perhaps he needed to wander for a while longer. In the Navy for twenty years, he had perfected not staying in one place.

"You sure this is all right?" Tony asked him. "And what about Panzer?" He reached down and rubbed his dog under the chin.

"I own the place. The dog's fine. Please. You'll like Bend. It's high desert. It'll be a nice change of pace."

What he meant was that it would take his mind off the ocean and what had happened there years ago.

"What the hell."

They shook hands, embraced, and then Tony watched his old friend trudge back through the grass to the parking lot.

Crouching down toward his dog, Tony wrapped his hands behind its cropped ears, which stood straight up, alert.

"What do you think, Panzer? You've never seen much snow."

The schnauzer cocked its head to the side, its brows raised.

"That's what I thought."

The two of them headed off down the trail toward Yachets.

CHAPTER 2

The knock on the door came four days after Tony had gotten to Bend. It was late Friday night, and he was lounging in Joe Pellagreno's condo hot tub, his eyes closed, drinking a local microbrew and trying his best to soak away the pain from a crash he had taken while snow shoeing near Mt. Bachelor earlier in the afternoon.

His Uncle Bruno had always told him to never answer the phone or the door after dark. No good news came at that time.

Now the door bell buzzed and his dog finally jumped from its bed and plodded across the hardwood floor toward the commotion, stopping a few feet from the door in a pose that would have won him a championship at a dog show.

Reluctantly, Tony got out, toweled off and made his way to the door, the towel protecting his nakedness.

Looking through the peephole, he saw Cliff Humphrey for the first time in person.

Tony opened the door.

Humphrey was a tall man in his early fifties, his gray Armani suit impeccable.

"Mr. Caruso?"

"Joe said you'd be here days ago," Tony said.

"I've had some business in Portland," he said, and then he half-smiled with his perfect, bleached teeth. "May I come in?"

Panzer growled and Humphrey took a step backward.

"Panzer. *Schlafen da!*" The dog immediately followed Tony's order, padding back and laying down on its bed near the warmth of the gas fireplace.

Tony assessed the man carefully. Humphrey's only imperfections were bloodshot eyes and an odor of alcohol about him. But considering his son had died recently, those were probably only temporary afflictions.

"Come in," Tony said. Having the man sit down, Tony went into his bedroom and slipped on a pair of shorts. When he returned, Humphrey was still sitting where he put him, his hands folded across his lap as if he were praying.

"Want a beer?"

Humphrey didn't answer, so Tony took a seat across from him and waited. He had learned patience in the military, standing in line like Russians waiting for something that never came, or when it did come it was never what you expected or wanted.

"You know about my son's death recently?" Humphrey finally said, his thin lips barely moving as he spoke.

Tony's dark eyes sunk deep into the man across from him. "Joe told me about the murder suicide over at the Cascade Peaks Estates. From what they say, your son blew the shit outta some perfectly good real estate." Too harsh? Maybe.

Seemingly unfazed, Humphrey got up and went to the balcony door, gazing across the dark thirteenth fairway at the lights of the city below. A cool breeze flowed through the sliding glass door, bringing the distinct smell of juniper with it.

"That's the story the sheriff has spread to the media," Humphrey said over his shoulder.

Tony got up and went to the refrigerator. "You want a beer?" he asked Humphrey again.

When the man didn't look his way, Tony shrugged and opened a local microbrew, taking a healthy swig of India Pale Ale as he walked over to the man, the chill of night air bringing goose bumps to Tony's exposed skin.

"What do you want from me?" Tony asked him.

Turning swiftly, Humphrey looked confused and possibly vulnerable. Two things completely unfamiliar to the man, Tony guessed.

"Joe told me your son wouldn't kill a fly. And he sure as hell wouldn't kill himself. You think someone killed him. The whole thing made to look like a murder suicide."

Humphrey's eyes brightened. "Yes. That's exactly it."

"Great. How do you think I can prove that?"

Humphrey glanced about the room. "This will be my first Christmas alone," he said, his thoughts off subject.

Tony had done a quick background check on Humphrey, and knew about his wife dying last January when she was thrown from her horse east of Prineville. That was a double dose of bad luck for one year. First the wife; now the son.

"I'm sorry for your loss," Tony said. He took a drink of beer and said, "What do you want me to do?"

"Find out the truth about my son. I know he didn't do this. Sure, he and Barb were having problems. But what young couple doesn't have a few bumps in their marriage."

"His gun was found at his side. What if I find out he did it?"

Humphrey let out a deep breath, as if that could be the last possible outcome. "Then I'll have to start accepting that fact. But I know he didn't. I understand you worked with the police as a consultant after retiring from the Navy. Maybe you could check over the scene, talk with the sheriff." He hunched his shoulders. It was obvious the man was out of his element, and that bothered him. Control was everything to this man.

"I'll need some cash," Tony finally said. "Make the whole thing professional. You've checked me out, so you know my fees. If the hours add up, I'll also need a week in September on the Oregon coast." For the last few jobs Tony had taken, he had gotten a week of timeshare at an Oregon resort for his services. Many people in the west had collected timeshares over the past two decades like stamps, and now found them as useless as internet stocks.

Humphrey nodded agreement and then pulled out his wallet and counted off ten crisp one hundred dollar bills. He handed them to Tony, who folded them into his back pocket.

"If you need more just ask," he said. "I want to know what's going on. Call me at this number at least once a day." He handed Tony his card with a business number and address for Bend and Portland. Below that he had scribbled another number. Probably a cell phone.

"I'll ask a few questions," Tony said, shrugging. "But nine times out of ten these things are exactly as they appear."

"Not this time, Mr. Caruso." He headed toward the door but stopped before leaving and turned back to face Tony. "And I want total anonymity. Tell no one who you're working for."

"No problem." Tony opened the door for him.

Humphrey started out and stopped again. He retrieved an envelope from inside his suit and handed it to him. "That's a pass card for Cascade Peaks Estates, and some things that will acquaint you with my son and his wife. Might come in handy. I have your e-mail address and cell phone number, and, of course, Joe's number here."

After Humphrey left, Tony went over to the balcony and looked out onto the city lights, thinking a good portion of those were probably there because of Cliff Humphrey. He had a bad feeling about this case. It was stuck down in his gut fighting it out with the India Pale Ale. Maybe he should have listened to his Uncle Bruno and stayed in the hot tub.

His dog came to his side and rubbed his head against Tony's bare leg. Panzer was a good judge of character, and even he had growled. Great.

Right now, at that moment, he wondered how it would be floating in the frigid waters of the Pacific.

CHAPTER 3

Tony got up the next morning bright and early. It was another clear, crisp December day on the high desert. According to the weather guru on the local morning radio show, the temps would reach the mid-fifties.

Bend, as Tony had quickly learned in the past few days, was a town of two sides, split down the middle by the Deschutes River—a world-class trout fishery, kayak Mecca and star of John Wayne westerns. The east side was Bend's past, with small bungalows inhabited by the working class who built high-end Pozzi windows and RVs for the uber-rich. The west side was new Bend—million-dollar houses in gated golf communities—houses owned by displaced Californians and second home owners from Portland and Seattle. Equity movers and shakers.

Drinking his second cup of coffee zapped in the microwave, Tony sat down at the kitchen table and opened the envelope Cliff Humphrey had given him the night before. There was the pass card to the gate at the Humphrey sub-division, copies of identification cards, credit cards, social security cards, and photos of Dan Humphrey and his wife, Barb. They had the looks of the college football quarterback and the star volleyball player. An inside hitter.

Now he was almost ready to hit the road. But before he left, he checked his e-mail. He had a web page posted to links all over the place where he offered discreet investigations nationwide, with

Oregon his home base. He mentioned his Navy ordnance training and the work he had done as a consultant with the police, but gave little specific information. Strangely enough, he also had a link to a photo gallery—maybe some would see he had a softer side, and had not just worked with bombs most of his life.

He had a couple of messages. The first one was from Melanie Chadwick, a woman he had dated a couple of times since coming to Bend. They had met his first day in town at a local gym where Tony was working out. Since then they had spent a lot of free time searching for bodily imperfections. He was no doctor, but he had found nothing physically wrong with her.

The other message was from his Uncle Bruno in Duluth, Minnesota, wanting to know when he was coming home again. He left Melanie hanging for now and shot off a quick reply to his uncle, saying he had no intention of ever going back to Minnesota in the winter. Although he had grown up in Duluth's west end, a place where Italian names were as common as hockey rinks, he had forced himself to return only infrequently during the summer. Since leaving Duluth after high school to serve in the Navy, traveling the Earth for more than 20 years, he hadn't found much time to return to Minnesota. He had a feeling his Uncle Bruno wanted him to take over the family business, and Tony had only an inkling of what he had in mind for him. Bruno could have asked Tony's brother, Johnny, but last he heard his younger brother was in China teaching English to the newly affluent. Or was he in Africa with the Peace Corps?

"Let's go, boy," Tony said, snapping his fingers at his dog, who scurried toward the door after him. "Let's put that nose to work."

He left and found his ten-year-old Ford F250 in the one-car garage that came with the condo. The 4x4 was his office. His cell phone hitched up to his laptop, and he had a bed in the back that he could use in emergencies. Next to his bed was a pad for Panzer.

Leaving the resort, he headed south toward Cascade Peaks Estates.

Since it was Saturday, there wasn't much traffic at that time of day. The skiers were probably already on the slopes, and the diehard golfers were eating brunch, lying about their handicaps while they waited for the greens to warm.

Most detectives would head directly to the local cops and ask to see the evidence. Have them explain their reasoning for calling it quits on a case that wasn't a total slam dunk. But Tony figured that was a good way to piss people off. Sort of like asking an older man if he could still get it up.

Besides, he wanted to take a look at what was left of Dan and Barb Humphrey's house. He had heard that Dan had somehow rigged the gas fireplace in the living room to explode. Details on the local T.V. news and in the newspaper were sketchy at best. Cryptic at most. The Bend area being such a tourist Mecca, it was best to keep any negative news to a minimum, Tony guessed.

He made it through the gate with Cliff's card without the resort Gestapo jacking him up against his truck. The stern man in the gatehouse did burn his eyes right through him, though. He realized his dented and beat-up pickup didn't fit in with the Beemers, Mercedes and Audis strolling around that gated community. Screw 'em. Tony actually used his four-wheel-drive for something more than status.

Finding the house was not a difficult task. It was the only place on the golf course that resembled a burnt marshmallow.

He got out, followed closely by Panzer, and stood for a moment, surveying the scene, when he noticed the curtains pulled back from the closest neighbor's side window on the second floor. He pulled his camera from the passenger seat, slung it over his right shoulder, and closed the door, ignoring the neighbor.

He had been through more than a few fried dwellings. Luckily, this time, he wouldn't trip over some crispy critter.

Strange. There were no yellow police tapes saying not to be there. Yet, on the golf course side, a tall wooden fence had been hastily erected so those golfers with delicate sensibilities would-

n't have to look at the torched house and think about what had
happened there.

Stepping through the blackened mess, he took a few photos and
made his way to what he guessed had been the living room. There
had been a massive picture window that was gone now. The white
Berber carpeting was crystallized black and crunched under his
feet with each step. The odor of smoke drifted up, tweaking his
nostrils. Smells linger in your mind longer than any other sense,
he knew. For a slight moment he was in the Sumatran village trying to figure out how one of his Navy pilots had mistaken it for
the real target a few miles to the south. Then even farther back,
he was searching through his family house after his little brother
had set the place ablaze, searching for a dog that would eventually look like a pig on a luau spit.

Panzer made his way through the room and was now on his
stomach, his broad head resting on his front paws and his eyes
pointing directly at the fireplace.

Moving across the large opening, Tony stopped next to the
black stone fireplace. Rocks had fallen to the floor from the
explosion. He took a few more shots at wide angle, not needing
a flash, since the ceiling to the second floor had been blown half
way to Boise and light streamed in from the opening in the roof
that had burned through. He picked around for a moment, but he
guessed the police had removed any evidence of importance.
Shifting his eyes across the floor, he could see where the two
bodies had fallen, their flesh having preserved a small swatch of
carpet. He took close ups of those areas.

"You got a good nose, Panzer," he said, patting his dog on the
head. "*Sitzen.*"

The dog immediately rose up and sat next to him.

Then Tony saw it. It wasn't much. In fact, to the untrained eye,
nothing at all would have registered. But tucked alongside the
base of the bottom stone to the right of the fireplace opening was
a tiny piece of wiring no more than an inch in length. He picked
up the little yellow plastic coating, with a red stripe that ran

lengthwise, and twirled it in his fingers, examining it more close-ly. It was melted and charred at the tip, but the bottom stones had sheltered the wire from the blaze. He shoved it into his front pocket. Considering the obvious explosion and resulting fire, it was amazing that anything had survived the intense heat. Glancing around the room one more time, he headed out.

He didn't expect to find much, and he didn't disappoint him-self.

Next, he put Panzer in the back of the truck and then walked over to the neighbor's place and knocked on the thick oak door. No answer.

He stepped back and looked up to the second floor. A woman was there, but she darted back when she saw him.

This time he rang the doorbell. Still nothing.

Tony started to walk down the driveway, when a truck pulled up and two men jumped out. They were both bulky bouncer types, dressed in brown uniforms with silver badges sewn on the chest. On their thick biceps was a patch that read, "Cascade Peaks Security."

Adjusting the camera at his waist, Tony snapped off a shot of them at wide angle as they approached. Something for his web-site maybe.

The two men got closer and stopped, widening their stance like sailors do on a ship in high seas. The one on the left had a blond flattop. He was at least six two, four or five inches taller than Tony, but his midsection was soft. The one on the right was five or six inches shorter, but had more bulk. His hair was stringy black in a floppy surfer cut. He had a scar from his upper lip to his nose, covered slightly by a goatee. Hell of a shaving accident.

Tony started to say something, when the one with the goatee reached for him.

Tony blocked away the man's arm, and now Panzer started barking from inside the truck.

Flattop pulled his nightstick. Tony caught his arm, twisted it around, and elbowed him in the jaw. The man fell to his knees.

Then Tony took the club from Flattop and jabbed it into the
sternum of the advancing Goatee, sending him gasping backwards.

"What the fuck?" Tony said, adjusting his camera on his shoulder. "Just hold it before someone gets hurt."

Flattop was on his knees, his mouth bleeding. He reached for
his gun. Tony grabbed his arm and twisted it back, slamming him
to the ground onto his shoulders.

Tony was wrestling with him when Goatee started whacking
him with his stick. He took three or four blows before rolling
over and kicking the stick from the man's hand.

Now Tony was pissed. The guy could have hit his camera, and
he had a feeling one of his ribs was broken, but he had no time to
check it out.

He hopped up and kicked Goatee with a roundhouse to his ribs.
Then followed that with a side thrust kick to his stomach, sending him flailing backwards.

When Tony turned for the other man, Flattop had his gun drawn
and pointed right at Tony's head.

Tony froze.

"Think hard before pulling the trigger," Tony said. Looking at
the guy more closely, he was probably just barely a legal drinker.

"Put that gun away, Ricky."

All three of them turned to see a black man in his fifties
approaching. His short hair was speckled with gray. He was tall
with thick shoulders and had the start of a nice beer gut, like pro
football offensive linemen carry to push defensive ends around.
On the shoulders of his uniform were captain's bars on each
epaulet.

The Flattop rent-a-cop did what his boss said.

"Sir, we got a report of a suspicious character peeking into windows," Flattop said, nodding his thick skull toward Tony.

The captain laughed. "Look at him. Both of you."

They did as the captain said.

"Clean shaven. Nice clothes. What in the hell made you think he was some kinda burglar?"

They thought it over.

"Sorry, sir," Flattop said.

"Not to me," the captain said. "To him."

Flattop cast his reluctant eyes on Tony. "Sorry," he said, the word painful and strained.

Tony nodded. The captain was right, Tony didn't look like much of a threat. That had always been his plan. Made it easier to surprise people.

"Good thing I'm not litigious," Tony said to the two young and over-zealous rent-a-cops. They stared at him with stupid expressions, and Tony imagined one of them would eventually look up the word in the dictionary and see how close they had come to being sued for assault.

The captain swished his head, and the two men pulled their tails between their legs and went back to the truck.

After the two junior park rangers took off, the captain pulled Tony aside and introduced himself as Beaver Jackson. Tony gave him his name, nothing else.

"Did you play football for OSU?" Tony asked.

The captain laughed. "Yeah. Centuries ago. Played a little pro ball up in Canada for a few years also. Until each knee had two operations."

The man had a slight twinkle in his eyes when he talked about football. The glory days.

"How'd you get the name Beaver?" Tony asked, trying to lighten the moment.

"Grew up in Portland. Real name is Balthasar. I paid a guy in high school to come up with a nickname. When I got a scholarship to OSU, he started calling me Beaver."

"Balthasar. One of the three wise men," Tony said.

"You know your bible," he said. "My mother was a fanatic about it."

"I'm a recovering Catholic," Tony said. "Twelve-step program."

They stared at each other for a moment. Finally, the captain said, "What are you doing at Cascade Peaks, Mr. Caruso?"

"I'm an insurance investigator," Tony said, starting the lie. "Looking into the alleged murder suicide next door. Can you give me your take on the situation?"

The man shifted his deep, dark eyes toward the nice house behind them, and then settled on Tony. "It was a tragic accident."

"Accident?"

"Well. Some people should know when to call it quits before things like this happen."

"Did you know Dan and Barb Humphrey?" Tony asked.

"I know everybody here. That's my job. We've got a few movie stars living here. A couple of professional athletes. They want their privacy. Security. This is private property, or maybe you didn't read the signs at the front gate."

He had read them. They were more elaborate than the Bill of Rights. "I understand privacy. But you didn't really answer my question. I need to clear the books on this case. Determine if we're going to pay off. You understand."

The captain laughed. "Yeah, I do. I understand you came through my gate with a pass card. If you're an insurance investigator, how'd you get that?"

Tony tried a smile and said, "Insurance companies have some pull."

Beaver Jackson let out a breath of air and then said, "I knew Dan and Barb. God has a way of making things right. They were a bit wild. Maybe that put a strain on their marriage."

"Wild? In what way?"

The captain stared at Tony. "Leave it alone, Mr. Caruso. Their death was a tragedy. This is a good community."

Tony wasn't going to get any more out of Captain Beaver Jackson. At least not now. "I do need to talk with the neighbors. It's routine. You understand."

From the look on the man's face he didn't. But he said, "I guess. But maybe I should accompany you."

"People tend to talk more openly when there isn't a uniform involved," Tony said. Which is one reason every police department in America had detectives in plain clothes.

Beaver Jackson pointed his thick finger at Tony. "Don't go disturbing these people. Their property values have taken a hit."

Tony tried not to smile. Property values? He sounded like the Chamber of Commerce.

The rent-a-captain didn't seem to like it much, but he backed away and drove off. Tony had a feeling he wouldn't go far. He checked his camera. Not a scratch or dent on it. He wished he could say the same for his back ribs, which ached with each step he took toward the large wooden door. Maybe the lady of the house would answer this time.

CHAPTER 4

The neighbor with the best view of Dan and Barb Humphrey's place lived in an elaborate stone and wood structure that looked more like a Scottish hunting estate than a residence in the high desert of Oregon. It was five thousand square feet of pure opulence. Since it was winter now, it was hard to tell the true nature of the landscaping. But Tony imagined it was something quite splendid in mid-summer; groomed, trimmed and weeded by those who lived east of the river.

Having seen Tony scuffle with the two rent-a-cops in her front yard, and then later talking with the security captain like old friends, the lady of the house must have decided it was all right to talk with him. She answered the door just as he raked his knuckles on the elaborate carved wood.

"Whatever it is, I'm not buying," said the woman before the door was completely open. "Besides, don't you know it's against our covenants to solicit door-to-door in Cascade Peaks?"

Deciding how to respond, Tony's eyes scanned the woman top to bottom. She wore black exercise tights and an aerobics top that barely held back her almost-too-perfect breasts.

Finally, he held out his hand and said, "Tony Caruso. I'm an insurance investigator looking into what happened next door."

She let his hand hang there. "Mrs. James Ellison." With that, she turned and started walking away, her tall, slim figure accentuated with each step she took. Suddenly, she stopped and turned sideways, her eyes inspecting him top to bottom. "Are you coming?"

He entered and closed the door behind him. As he followed her, he tried to guess her age, but was coming up blank. He guessed early fifties, but she could have easily passed for ten years younger. With her streaked blonde hair and near-perfect physique, the task was almost impossible.

She ushered him in through a wide vestibule with Italian marble floors and exposed oak beams. They reached a solarium with lavish tropical plants set atop a large flagstone floor. They sat at a glass-topped wrought iron table overlooking a wooden deck that had a nice view of the fifth green. An indoor waterfall trickled delicately in one corner. The deck alone had more square footage than the average American home, Tony noticed.

"Would you like some tea or coffee?" she asked.

She spoke like an actress in a movie, trying with all her power to cover up a southern accent.

"Thanks. But I've had my limit for the day. I'm afraid I get a little hyper with too much."

"I saw that on my lawn." Her eyes shot down his body and rested on his pants.

Looking down, Tony noticed for the first time grass stains on both knees of his new khakis. Those wouldn't come out easy.

"A misunderstanding," Tony said, hunching his shoulders.

She let out a slight chuckle. Then she raised a plate with white pastries on it.

"How about a scone?" she asked.

Reluctantly, he picked one up and took a bite out of it. It crumbled slightly, dropping specks to the glass top and his pants.

Between bites, Tony asked, "What can you tell me about your former neighbors, Dan and Barb Humphrey?"

She hesitated long enough to pour herself a cup of tea and sip it delicately. Then she leaned back and crossed her shapely legs.

"They were a nice couple. Dan was quite the lady killer. I'm sorry. I didn't mean it that way."

Her face turned completely red. He waited for her to recover.

"I meant," she started again, picking her words more carefully, "that he was handsome. Dark like you, but taller. Although his shoulders weren't as broad as yours. He didn't have your strong build."

"What about Barb?" he asked. Then he shoved the rest of the scone into his mouth.

"She was beautiful. Smooth auburn hair. A milky complexion. Had a body that any man would love to see, and any woman would kill to have."

Cliff Humphrey had included the photos of Dan and Barb in the folder. He knew how they looked, but that didn't tell him what he really needed to know.

He swallowed the last of the scone and then asked, "Were they a happy couple?"

She thought about that. "Dan killed her and then blew himself to pieces. How happy could they be?"

He decided to come from another angle. "Think back before this happened. What was your impression of them then?"

She gave it some heavy thought. Her soft blue eyes shifted about as if scanning back through her brain for a file. Finally she said, "I thought they had an interesting marriage. Not perfect. But surely not a violent one."

He knew that this was the answer nearly every neighbor gave after a domestic murder suicide. It was as if the neighbors couldn't have seen any problems or they would be partially to blame for not intervening. Yet, he didn't think that's how Mrs. Ellison was thinking. She believed what she was saying.

"You said interesting," he said. "How so?"

Now she had a girlish grin. She moved forward slightly as if she were telling him a secret. "They had some wild parties over there."

Wild. Both her and super captain had used that word. "Define wild."

"Naked Jacuzzi parties. They didn't think anyone would notice.

Or they didn't care. They'd walk around the side of their house with no clothes on. Even run through the golf course sprinklers at midnight like children. Screaming and giggling."

She sighed heavily. He wasn't sure if she had been disgusted by their actions, turned on, or jealous. Maybe all of the above.

"Did you ever attend any of them?" he asked her.

Before answering, she leaned back and crossed her legs again. She took a sip of tea and then set the cup back in the saucer without a sound. "I went to one. That's it."

"What happened?"

"I'm a married woman. My husband is ten years my senior. James was in Portland on business. Why am I telling you this?"

He shrugged and noticed the huge rock on her left ring finger for the first time.

She continued. "By the time I got there everyone was pretty inebriated or worse," she said. "It was a smaller party. Perhaps ten people. Shortly after I got there people started taking their clothes off and settling into the Jacuzzi. Others were screwing right on the back yard." She hesitated long enough to make sure he was looking directly at her eyes. "I'm not into the multiple partner thing."

"And the Humphrey's?"

"Anything went with them, I think."

"Did they try to involve you?"

"I'm not a total prude. But I simply watched. Barb did it with at least two men at a time. Dan was with more than one woman that I saw. It didn't seem to matter who was with whom. I left shortly after."

Tony considered what she had told him. He was cursed with a near photographic memory. It saved on paper and having to take notes, but it didn't serve him well when having to testify in court when he worked as a consultant for the police. He could never truthfully say he couldn't remember something.

"Did you know anyone else at the party?" he asked.

She thought about that. "Dawn Sanders was there. She was

always over there. I guess she was Barb's best friend."

He made a mental note of her name.

"Anyone else you knew?"

"I think Dan's business partner was also there. Larry Gibson."

Gibson was already on his list to visit.

"What can you tell me about the neighbors on the other side of the Humphrey's place?"

She shook her head swiftly. "You won't find anyone there. It's owned by some young basketball player. He only lives there in the off season."

She gave Tony the man's name, but he didn't recognize it. He hadn't followed the team much in the last few years.

Tony thanked her for the info, and she showed him to the door.

Before she closed the door, he thought of something. "What does your husband do, Mrs. Ellison?"

"He's a venture capitalist," she said proudly.

A very successful one at that, he thought. Then he asked, "Were you home the night the Humphrey's...died?"

"I was here watching television," she said calmly. "Alone."

"Didn't see anything out of the ordinary?"

She smiled. "Well, a house doesn't normally blow up like that, Mr. Caruso."

Okay. He had that coming.

She let him out and he walked back toward his truck. He got up to the window on the Leer bed topper, coming nose to nose with his dog.

"What do you think, Panzer?"

The dog whined and licked the screen.

"That's what I thought."

Getting into the cab, Tony sat back in the seat; his ribs ached. They were heavily bruised but not broken. He'd felt broken ribs in the Navy after an F-14 turned on the flight deck of his aircraft carrier and its exhaust bounced him ten feet down into a metal catwalk railing. Only the railing kept him from flying another seventy feet to the South China Sea. Would have been his second trip to the drink.

What had made those two rent-a-cops start whacking him? His Uncle Bruno always said that if a man punched him in the gut he should hit him twice in the mouth. Then go find his brother and do the same to him.

He took a drink of bottled water to wash down the remnants of the scone, and gazed at Mrs. Ellison's house. She was in the upstairs window again, not even trying to hide this time.

Tony drove off and noticed the security captain's truck parked down the road in the basketball player's driveway.

CHAPTER 5

The offices of Deschutes Enterprises sat on a ridge overlooking the Deschutes River six blocks from the old downtown of Bend. A few years back the entire area was a field of
sagebrush, lava rock and noxious weeds. Now there were new
stone and brick and wood structures filled with high tech companies, hotels, and real estate agencies. Clean companies, unlike the
old heritage of the city, which was built by the lumber industry
hacking up the Cascades old growth forests. All that remained of
that former time was three tall smoke stacks and a few converted
warehouses that were now trendy shops and specialty coffee
houses.

Being Saturday, only a few cars sat in the parking lot, the most
distinguished being a dark blue metallic Audi TT, with the hard
top, in a designated spot close to the front entrance. The car had
vanity Oregon Salmon license plates that read, 'Gibs.' It looked
like Tony was in luck.

Deschutes Enterprises was housed on the top floor of a three
story structure in a leased space in a stone-brick building with
tinted windows facing Mount Bachelor. Conceivably, with the
proper optics, one could watch the skiers on a clear day some
eighteen miles to the west.

Tony was ushered into the office of Larry Gibson by a pretty,
young receptionist with a nose ring and a mini skirt highlighting
legs that were, more than likely, honed to perfection by cross

country skiing and mountain biking. Her silky brown hair hung straight down her back, stopping just above her thin waist.

"Would you like some coffee?" she asked him, her smile sincere.

"Thanks, but I've had my morning limit."

She nodded and left him alone in the office.

It was a nice space. Not elegant, but functional. A large white L-shaped desk sat in the corner window with a state-of-the-art computer, its screen saver flipping through various Star Trek scenes. Tony wasn't sure how anyone could get work done with such a view of the river and mountain.

To the right of the desk sat a cherry credenza with a few trophies and plaques. On the wall behind that was a set of framed photographs. Tony noticed one with Dan and Barb Humphrey and another man, whom he assumed was Larry Gibson. They were at a Cascade lake standing in front of a sail boat. Barb was wearing a bikini, and Dan and Larry were on either side of her, their arms locked behind her head.

"How may I help you?" Gibson said, walking in and standing in the center of the room.

He was at least six-two with a slim tennis physique. Tan Dockers with brown deck shoes. A pink polo shirt was covered by a v-neck wool sweater. His thinning blond hair was cut short and he had the start of crow's feet to the side of each blue eye, making him look slightly older than his thirty-two years.

"I work for an insurance interest," Tony said. Hell, you start a lie, it's best to stick with it.

They took seats in leather chairs, Gibson pulling his closer to Tony. Too close.

"What exactly does Deschutes Enterprises do?" Tony asked. For people he didn't know, he liked to ask a question or two for which he already knew the answer. Like a lie detector, he would get a baseline for a truthful facial expression. Then when he was fed crap he'd recognize it for what it was.

Gibson chewed on the question, along with a new wad of gum

he had just shoved in his mouth. Finally he said, "We do a lot of things. We develop software programs for the entertainment industry. We build high end web sites, although not many. We've developed computer architecture for faster computing. Just got a patent on our newest design. We also have consultants who travel throughout the Pacific Northwest helping small businesses with their computing needs. We're very diversified."

"Sounds like it," Tony said. He pulled out a small notebook and flipped through as if looking for something. Some people have a hard time believing in pure memory, so he indulged them with at least pretending to take notes.

"What exactly are you looking for, Mr. Caruso? Susie said something about insurance. I have all the insurance I need."

Perfect opening. "Did you have a policy on Dan Humphrey?"

Gibson's brows rose, and then he recovered with a slight smile, his gum smacking through an open mouth. "What are you getting at?"

"Do you always answer a question with a question?"

"What do you think?" Gibson laughed at himself.

Great. A fucking comedian. "I take it you were Dan Humphrey's best friend," Tony said, studying the man carefully.

"We were business partners," he said. "We started this company out of my parent's garage after graduating from OSU."

"Regular Gates and Allen."

"I wish," he said wistfully, narrowing his eyes toward Tony. Smack the gum.

"About the partnership," Tony said. "When Dan died, you gained complete control of this company. I imagine that's a lot of money."

"I don't understand." He looked disturbed, shifting positions in the chair, and gulping down a spot of spit.

"Did you have partnership insurance on Dan?"

Gibson thought for a moment. "Are you with the police? If not, you can leave now."

"I told you I represent an insurance interest," Tony said. "If you don't want to collect the policy Dan took out on himself..." Tony got up and started for the door.

Gibson followed him. "Just a minute. I'm sorry. It's just that Dan's death was very difficult for me. We were room mates in college. I was the best man at his wedding. It's hard to believe he did what he did." He hesitated, looking rather confused. "We took out a policy on each other, but it had a suicide clause. So I, this company, gets nothing from his death."

"I see." Tony realized he should have known everything about every insurance policy Dan and Barb Humphrey had ever taken out. Luckily he was good at playing catch up.

They took seats again.

Time to get more personal. "What about Barb?" Tony asked.

Before answering, Gibson spit his gum into a trash can at the side of his desk. "She was also an employee here, but we didn't have a policy out on her."

"What did she do?"

"She was our marketing director."

"That's quite a loss," Tony said. "Losing your partner and your marketing director in one day."

Gibson was rattled again. "They were my friends! I've hardly had time to consider how their deaths will affect the company. I've been grieving for their loss."

"I'm sorry. So you totally buy what the police are saying? You really think Dan shot his wife and then blew himself up in his five hundred thousand dollar house on the fifth green of Cascade Peaks Estates?"

He raised both hands and hunched his shoulders. "I guess so. What else could it be?"

"Sure. I understand they were about to call it quits on the marriage. Is that right?"

"I wouldn't know."

Finally, the crap meter spiked. "I heard they had an open marriage. If you know what I mean." Tony gave him his best smirk.

Gibson shrugged. "No, I don't."

Tony moved uncomfortably close to Gibson. "Heard they liked
to do it with other people, while the other one watched."

Gibson jumped to his feet. "That's total bullshit! Get out." His
long skinny finger pointed toward the door, his face red and his
jaw clenched.

Slowly rising from his chair, Tony went to the door. He stopped
and smiled at Larry Gibson. "Where were you the night Dan and
Barb were barbecued?"

Calmly, the red from Gibson's face finally cleared, and he said,
"I don't have to answer shit!" Pause. "Home. Asleep. By myself."

"When I find out both of them were murdered, I expect to collect a percentage of their policies from you. How much are you
willing to give up?"

The man's jaw dropped, speechless.

Tony nodded his head, tapped his pen against his notebook, and
drifted out the door. "Have a nice day," he said over his shoulder.

On his way out the front door, Tony smiled at the receptionist,
and went out toward his truck. He thought about alibis. Being
single like Larry Gibson, he guessed he was without an alibi six
out of seven nights a week, drinking beer and eating pizza. He
couldn't hold that against anyone.

Thinking about the morning, Tony guessed it had gone better
than expected. He had managed to get bruised ribs, and followed
that up with bruising Gibson's ego. Maybe he was a little too hard
on the guy, but that's the way Tony liked to work. Piss them off
early and appologize later. It was the Navy way.

♦

Squeezed between two cars in the back row of the parking lot,
the driver of the black Ford Ranger pickup truck cranked over the
engine and put it in gear.

The driver looked into his rearview mirror, ran his hand across
his flattop, and then settled his eyes for a moment on his fat lip.
"That fuckin' bastard's gonna pay for this," the man said to his

friend in the passenger seat.

"Just keep your eyes on that F-Two-Fifty," the man with the goatee said. "You're just pissed cuss I got ta whack him a few times with my night stick."

The driver turned out onto the side street, keeping way back from the Ford.

"Dude, next time it's my turn to crank on his ass."

They kept far back. With the light Saturday traffic, it was no problem following the F250.

CHAPTER 6

It was almost noon. Whereas it was somewhat surprising to find Larry Gibson at the office on a Saturday, the opposite was true in the case of Melanie Chadwick. As a real estate broker with any desire at all to make sales, she would work the weekends when most people were off to look at houses.

Three Sisters Realty was located just two blocks from Deschutes Enterprises in a new log and stone structure on a landscaped precipice overlooking a rapid part of the Deschutes River. The outside plants, juniper, manzanita and various natural sagebrush, were positioned precisely along a curving cobblestone sidewalk. Landscaping had to be a booming business in Central Oregon, Tony thought.

Tony stopped in to see if Melanie wanted to do lunch, but a young receptionist told him she was hosting an open house from one to three. She gave him the address.

On the way to the house on Bend's westside, Tony picked up a couple of sub sandwiches at a downtown deli. He parked on the street and started toward the door, stopping to check out the sell sheet attached to the real estate sign, his eyes glancing sideways up and down the street.

"Shit," he mumbled softly. "Four hundred grand for two thousand square feet? Hope that comes with a live-in maid."

He got to the door and knocked. All he could hear was the baying of beagles from the neighbor's yard.

Finally, the door swung in.

"Hey, lady, does this place come with the fuckin' beagles?"

"What are you doing here?" Melanie asked, as Tony walked past her carrying the paper bag lunch.

"I figured you'd be too busy getting ready for the open house to remember to eat lunch."

She was alone in the place. It was a newer house in a hilly section of town nestled among a grove of two hundred year old ponderosa pines.

"You didn't have to do that," she said. "See, I have cookies and coffee." She waved her hand elegantly like a game show babe. At five-nine, the two of them looked eye-to-eye. Wearing a conservative gray skirt that hugged her hips, she obviously kept herself in great shape by doing all things physical. The two of them had sparred in martial arts a few times in the past couple of days at the gym, and she had held her own.

He raised the bag. "I got you a six-inch ham and cheese, no onions."

"I wish I didn't have to settle for six inches," she said, running her hand to the back of his neck. "And I was hoping for Italian sausage."

"This place has three bedrooms."

She checked her watch. "Damn. People always show up early to these things. Let's go out tonight. The Riverfront. A little wine. We could go back to my place. Or the condo. Your choice."

"Sounds good."

They ate the sandwiches without saying a word, and washed it down with a glass of water.

"Do you know a developer in town named Cliff Humphrey?" Tony asked.

Her head bolted up. "Of course. I know all the developers in town. He has an office in Bend, but he's from Portland. Why do you ask?"

"What do you know about him?"

She gave him one of her serious quizzical looks. The kind she did when her mind was racing fast to keep up with her words. "Humphrey and a few other Valley developers bought up a lot of land around Bend more than a decade ago," she said. "They must have known the area would start growing like this. They've put in subdivisions all over town, including the place you're staying."

He already knew most of this. "What about Cascade Peaks Estates?"

She thought for a second. "Yeah. That's one of theirs. I understand they're getting ready to build a new destination resort on five hundred acres a mile west of here. The home-site views will be spectacular. There will be a championship eighteen hole golf course. Olympic pool. Stables. Tennis courts. Fitness center. The lots alone will go for two fifty. That is if they can get the land use permit."

"Is that a problem?"

She laughed. "Usually nothing is a problem for Humphrey and his friends. But this time they've run into a couple of snags. They need to buy an easement from Mount Jefferson Drive, and they need water rights."

"That's a problem."

"Why do you ask about Humphrey?"

He wasn't sure if he should involve her in what he was looking into, but she had lived in Bend for nearly ten years, so she was his only real friend there. And he had only known her for a couple of days.

"He hired me to look into his son's death."

"You're kidding, right? You heard his son Dan killed his wife, Barb, and then blew himself up."

"That's the story."

"You don't believe that's what happened?"

"I don't know. I told Cliff Humphrey I'd look into it. Did you know the two of them?"

"Is this an interrogation?" She smiled at him and crossed her arms over her chest.

"Of course not. You just called them Dan and Barb like you knew them."

She hesitated. "I sold them their house a few years back. I'd see them around town. Didn't really know them well. They hung out at different places. A little wild from what I hear."

There was that word again. Wild. "Wild? How so?"

"Nothing I can tell you first hand. Just rumors. I heard they liked to have clothing optional Jacuzzi parties."

"Interesting. Anyone you know attend one of those?"

"Actually, Barb asked me to a few of them. But I was always busy. My acupuncturist mentioned that she had been to one. Said if I was into the multiple partner thing I should give it a try."

"Acupuncture?"

"Yeah. It's great. Mostly for my injured knee. But she's helped me for a lot of things."

Tony thought about his ribs and wondered if she could heal the bruises around them.

He wanted to talk with her more about Dan and Barb. Find out if they had any other mutual friends. But people started showing up for the open house. She was right. They were at least fifteen minutes early. Would have been right around mid-coitus. Tony got the name of her acupuncturist and reminded Melanie they were on for that evening, before heading back to his truck.

Bend was a small town. It turned out the name Mrs. Ellison had given him as Barb Humphrey's best friend, and Melanie's acupuncturist were one and the same.

He'd always wanted to get poked by a thousand needles just for the hell of it.

Sitting out in his truck, his cell phone rang. Tony thought about letting it go to voice mail, but not many people knew his number, so it could have been important.

"Yeah," he said into the phone, his eyes scanning his rearview mirror.

"That's the way you answer your phone?" came a rough voice on the other end. Sounded like an old football coach.

"Uncle Bruno. How the hell's it hangin'?"

"Don't ask. Hey, you need to get your ass home for Christmas this year."

Tony didn't want to admit to his uncle that he didn't still consider Duluth his home. "You're still a crazy bastard," Tony said, his eyes focused on the road behind him. "What's the weather look like?"

"Fuck the weather, Tony boy. We got furnaces, you know. We got shit we need to discuss."

Uncle Bruno had two daughters. One married an Air Force doctor and was living in Japan. The other one was a federal prosecutor in Minneapolis, married to her two cats and struggling with her sexuality. Neither, as far as Tony knew, wanted anything to do with the family businesses.

"Uncle Bruno. I don't know shit about running a restaurant, a bar, or an import business."

"You're a quick study, Tony. Besides, there's more to it than that."

He had guessed there was, but maybe that's as obscure as he wanted it to be. "Let me think about it. Right now I've got a couple of lost puppies that might need a good ass whipping."

"See. That's what I'm talkin' about, Tony. Think it over."

With that, the phone went dead and Tony threw it to the passenger seat. He shook his head and turned over the engine. Pulling out slowly, he glanced back and saw the truck do the same thing.

CHAPTER 7

D awn Sanders lived in an older two story house a block from downtown Bend. It was a part of town where most of the original well-to-do had settled. Many of the houses had been converted into small businesses. Law firms. Accountants. Property managers. Quaint.

In the short time that Tony had been in Bend, he had learned that George Putnam, son of one of the New York publishing giants, had lived a few blocks away almost a century ago, and had run the local newspaper before moving on and eventually marrying Amelia Earhart.

The streets were narrow with cars parked on both sides. Large oaks, maples and pines shaded the yards. It was one of the only places in town where the cedar shake roofs actually had moss growing on them, since the sun rarely poked through the tall pines in the summer.

There was a modest sign out front of the white house that read, "Naturopathic Clinic." Below that was Dawn Sanders' name, followed by "Licensed Acupuncturist."

Tony had called her from his cell phone on the way over. Said he was a friend of Melanie Chadwick, and asked if she could see him on short notice. She had an interesting form of speech. Sort of a cross between unsubdued enthusiasm and laid back indifference. She said she wasn't open after noon on Saturday, but since he was Melanie's friend, she'd squeeze him in. He hoped she wasn't talking about her needles.

He got to the front door, unsure if he should knock or just walk in, since it appeared she lived there as well. He settled on a light knock.

Dawn Sanders answered the door wearing a flowered kimono. They shook hands and introduced each other. She had a firm shake. And she seemed to study him through her little round John Lennon spectacles. She looked about thirty-five, but could have been anywhere from twenty-five to forty. She was five-six with curly red hair spiraling to her narrow waist. As she walked away from him, ushering him through a waiting area, he could see she had nothing on under the draping kimono. And from his quick observation through back lighting, he could tell she worked out.

The inner room was part sterile doctor's office and part hippie smoke room. The lighting was subdued. The walls held framed posters of everything Asian. Landscapes of Chinese mountains. Peasants working flooded rice paddies. There were also charts of medicinal herbs and references to ancient uses for animal body parts. Tony's eyes settled on a diagram of the human body with pins poking from it like a giant voodoo doll.

"What ails you, Tony?"

Before he could answer, she put a CD into a player and transformed the room into the Far East. It reminded him of so many little shops he'd gone to in Singapore and Hong Kong. Then she lit some incense and turned back to him.

"Well?" she said.

"My neck has been giving me a lot of problems," he said. This wasn't a total lie. Ever since his accident on the aircraft carrier, where he had been blown to the catwalk, his neck had given him problems, especially when it rained. "And my back."

"Have you ever been to an acupuncturist, Tony?"

"No."

"Why not?"

He shrugged. "I don't know. Maybe I've never had a friend like Melanie who recommended one."

She gave him a nice smile. "Melanie is a beautiful woman. How long have you known her?"

"Just a couple of days."

"Are you new to Bend?"

As far as Tony could tell, this was a question almost everyone in Bend asked. From what he understood, it was an informal feeling out process. There had been so many newcomers to town, especially from California, that the older residents used it to find out where people were coming from, physically and mentally.

"I'm watching a friend's condo."

"So you're totally open to this?" she asked.

"Sure. Why not?"

"Take off your clothes and lay face down on the table."

Tony must have hesitated too long, because she smiled at him and handed him a gown.

"I'll give you a few minutes," she said. Then she left him standing there, wondering what in the hell he had gotten myself into this time.

Tony wasn't really the modest type. The military had a tendency of stripping away any reserve in people. So he did what Dawn Sanders said. He got into the gown, which had one of those back tying things impossible to reach. Then he lay on his stomach and waited. Seconds later she entered.

She got onto a rolling chair with a container in one hand, loaded with long skinny needles.

"I'll start with your neck," she said. She ran her strong fingers over the base of his skull. "Relax. You have a powerful neck."

"Umm... You have powerful hands."

"I work with my hands all day," she said. "I'm also a certified masseuse."

"That's wonderful."

"Now I'm going to start with the needles, so try to mellow out. You might feel a slight prick."

"That's what the teenage boy told his virgin girlfriend," Tony said.

She giggled like a little girl. "You have a nice sense of humor, Tony. That's important in life."

Whatever she was doing, it was working. Even though the pain had been minimal since coming to the dry high desert, he could feel improvement. Next she opened the back of the gown.

"Oh, my," she said. "You have fresh bruises back here."

"Yeah, I fell while show shoeing. Probably hit a tree limb under the snow."

She rubbed her hand on the outside of the bruised area, as if she knew exactly where the pain would be. Then Tony felt a few minor pin pricks. The pain didn't completely subside, but it was substantially less.

"How's that?" she asked.

He had his eyes closed now it felt so good. "Much better."

Tony was feeling so good, in fact, that he almost forgot he was there to ask her questions about Barb Humphrey. Then he was distracted further when she ran her hand across his bare butt.

"Do you have any pain here?" she asked.

"Should I say yes?"

"Only if it's true."

She settled her hand at his lower back, rubbed the skin gently between her fingers, massaged the muscle beneath that, and then seemed to hesitate.

"Relax," she said. "You're a strong guy, Tony. I can tell you use these more than most men."

For a slight moment he felt like a chunk of meat at a butcher shop with some woman squeezing the cellophane to see if he was fresh and tender. Nice cut.

"This isn't a bad thing," she continued. "You just need to learn how to let all the power within you escape."

He did what she said, trying his best to transform his body into a 190-pound pile of Jell-O. His best probably fell far short of what she had in mind, because she planted a few more needles in various locations around his buttocks. He didn't think about it then, but she could have done just about anything to him at that point and he wouldn't have complained. It was that relaxing. He also decided at that moment not to ask any questions about Dan and Barb Humphrey until she removed all her needles. He had a feeling she could bring pain as quickly as pleasure.

When she was done with his back side, having planted her needles from his neck to his heels, and then removed them as meticulously as she had placed them, she stood for a moment rubbing down his body.

"What about your front?" she asked. "Let's roll over and we'll see what we can do for you."

He immediately realized he had a problem that, although as a woman she was qualified to fix, an acupuncturist was not needed.

"Before we do," he said. "I was wondering about something."

She didn't say a thing. Instead, she crossed her arms to her chest and narrowed her glance his way.

"I understand you lost a good friend recently. Barb Humphrey?"

Cocking her head to one side, she said, "Yes. It was a terrible tragedy. Did you know Barb?"

"I'm afraid I didn't have the pleasure. I understand she was a very beautiful woman."

"She was."

"You were her best friend?"

She thought about it for a second. "I don't know how you judge that. We were very close."

"What about Dan?"

She stepped across the room and set her container of needles on a small table. Then she turned to him and simply stared.

"What's the matter?" Tony asked.

"Why do you want to know about Barb and Dan?"

"I'm with an insurance company," Tony said. He hated himself for lying to her. "I have to determine with one hundred percent certainty that Barb was murdered. You see, if it was as the local sheriff says, a murder suicide, then we will gladly pay Barb's beneficiary. Dan, on the other hand, committed suicide. So we won't pay that claim."

While he said this, her expression had flowed from somewhat quizzical to nearly complete reticence. And Tony felt like a complete asshole.

Finally she said, "I don't like being deceived, Mr. Caruso. If you wanted to know about Barb and Dan Humphrey, why didn't you just come and ask me? Don't come in here pretending you need an acupuncture treatment."

"I'm s—"

"I'm not done yet," she yelled. "I suppose you're not even a friend of Melanie's?"

Tony sat up quickly without thinking, and swiveled his bare feet to the floor. What he didn't know, was that his gown had stayed on the table.

She glanced down and raised her eyebrows. Then she smiled. "Your gown," she said.

He was slightly embarrassed, although not as much so if he have just stepped out of cold water. He wrapped the gown around his body.

There was a full minute where they both seemed suspended in time.

"I'm sorry," Tony said. "I'm just doing my job. Melanie is my friend. And, as you could see by my bruises, I thought acupuncture might help me with them."

She let out a deep breath and her disposition started to change back to her early cheerful self.

When she didn't say anything, Tony said, "You knew them both really well. Was Dan capable of killing Barb?"

She shrugged. "I don't know. Anything's possible."

"Had you ever seen him lose his temper?"

"No. He was always pretty mellow. Same with Barb. They were both pretty wild, though."

That word didn't want to go away. Tony seemed to be gaining her confidence again and didn't want to piss her off, but he needed to know something.

"I know about the parties they used to have at their house. The Jacuzzi. Everything." He tried to emphasize that last word with a knowing smile.

She returned his smile with a better one. "Those were a lot of fun," she admitted. "I don't know what you've heard about their parties, but the human body can be a beautiful thing when taken care of properly."

They stood there a bit uncomfortably, him more than her, since his bare butt was hanging out the back end.

"How was their relationship in the last week before they died?" Tony asked.

She thought for a long moment. "Barb was the same as always. Fun and games. Something was bothering Dan, but I don't think it had anything to do with Barb. She told me there was something wrong at work."

"Like what?"

"She didn't say."

"When was the last time you saw her?"

She thought hard. "We did lunch at The Bangkok the day she died. I love Thai food. Come to think of it, she was upset until she had a few glasses of Chardonnay."

"Did you see her after that?"

"She was at the Riverfront later that night. She was with Dan. They had another guy at their table. He looked kind of like you. He also had an Italian name, but I don't recall it now."

"They all left together?"

She nodded her head.

"What time was that?"

"Probably ten o'clock. I went home at eleven, so it had to be before then. Why is that important?"

He switched gears. "Did you mention this to the sheriff?"

"You're the first person to ask me the question."

Now that was interesting. Dan and Barb left a local bar with another man just two hours before all hell breaks loose at

Cascade Peaks Estates. That means there could have been a witness, or even more importantly, the third party could have done the both of them. In more ways than one.

"This Italian guy. Did you know him?"

"No," she said. "I saw him at the Riverfront a few times, but not since that night."

"You suppose they were going out for coffee somewhere?" he asked.

She laughed. "Yeah, right."

"So the trio goes back to Orgy Peaks, they have a little romp, and Dan gets jealous. Maybe Barb seems to be having entirely too much fun. They kick out the Italian stallion and start arguing. Except Dan goes overboard and actually kills her. Seeing what he's done. Distraught. He rigs the living room fireplace to blow the crap out of the place, burning him to a crispy critter in the process."

She had been shaking her head as he talked, and he knew it had something to do with his ludicrous reasoning. If he wasn't buying it, how in the hell could he expect anyone else to buy it? Even more importantly, why was the sheriff signing off on it?

"What?" Tony asked.

"They didn't worry about the other partner. It was strictly sex. They both got off on it. And besides, Dan always got his turn."

"He liked men, too?"

"No! He was definitely hetero. I meant one night they would pick up a guy, the next a woman."

"That's quite magnanimous of them," he said.

"They were that kind of people."

He had about everything he wanted to know from her, and some. Getting dressed in front of her didn't bother her in the least, and he figured she had already seen everything he had to offer.

When he was done they went to the front and he paid her for the session, adding a little extra for the information. She opened the door for him and Tony stepped onto the porch.

She shook his hand and held it for a moment. "If things don't work out with you and Melanie, give me a call." She smiled and handed him one of her cards.

He walked back and got into his truck. His dog in the bed started to whine. Panzer would need a run soon.

Tony hadn't noticed, but while he was in there getting poked with needles, a front had moved in with swirling clouds. The temperature had dropped to near freezing. Good thing he had his pants on.

Before pulling out, he glanced into his rearview mirror. A block and a half behind him was the black truck with his two friends from Cascade Peak Estates security. Still on his tail.

Tony smiled and pulled a U-turn, slowly drove up the lane and stopped alongside the black truck. Rolling down the window, he said, "Hey, guys. I'll be heading downtown to run a few errands, let the dog run. After that I'll probably go home and take a crap."

The two rent-a-cops seemed to sink down into their seats as Tony drove off.

He had to wonder why the two of them were following him around all morning. Although he had only started asking questions, he was making someone nervous. Break up the status quo. That was his motto.

CHAPTER 8

The silver Mercedes crept along the dirt road and turned left into the driveway. Cliff Humphrey parked just behind the old pickup truck with the back converted to compartments, the signs on the side indicating that explosives were inside.

He stepped out onto the dirt and immediately looked down at his black Italian loafers, which were instantly covered with powdery tan Central Oregon dust. He shook his left foot, but he knew that was useless. Letting out a deep breath, he moved forward gingerly.

Suddenly, the front door to the old house burst open and a scruffy-looking man with a long beard plodded out toward him.

"Get the fuck off my land!" the bearded man screamed, his right hand pointing down the road.

Humphrey stopped in his tracks in the middle of the driveway. "Just hear me out."

"Already heard your bullshit. Now get the fuck out."

Humphrey gazed about the property. He needed this. Calm and easy. "Listen. I'm sorry what happened to you. But you've got to believe me. . .I had nothing to do with it. That's not the way I work."

The other man grabbed his beard and stroked it, his eyes shifting wildly from side to side. "Why should I believe you?"

"Because it's the truth. And I think you understand that."

"I know one thing. You blackballed me in this town. I can't get no work." He swung his head back toward his house and shoved his thumb in that direction. "My grandparents built dis place damn near sixty years ago. You ain't gettin' it."

Humphrey racked his brain on how to deal with this guy. He had tried just about every tactic he knew. "The world has discovered Bend. There's no turning back on that. If it isn't me, it'll be someone else in a couple of years. I've offered you a fair price. More than fair. Now, I'm sorry your place was robbed, but I had nothing to do with that. You have to believe me."

The man struck a gaze at Humphrey, inspecting the swanky suit, the perfect hair, and the man's Mercedes, which, probably for the first time, had dust on its tires.

A cool breeze swept down out of the Cascades, and both men seemed to shiver.

A horse whinnied down a grade in a pasture out back. Both men turned to see a gray mare shifting its head up and down and then prancing about the small corral next to a decrepit shelter. The feisty Arabian glided across the ground, its tail pointing straight out.

"See, even your horse wants you to sell this place," Humphrey said smiling.

The man with the beard lifted his nose to the breeze. "Naw, she smells somethin' in the air. Could be a mountain lion. More likely your bullshit."

Humphrey turned and made his way back to the driver's door, opened it, and hesitated before getting in. "One way or another, you'll come to your senses. You'll deal with me." With that, he got into his car and started the engine. As he started to back out of the driveway, he shook his head as he noticed the man in his yard. He had turned around, bent over, and his pants were down at his ankles. His right index finger pointed at his hairy white cheeks.

♦

Tony had a feeling Dumb and Dumber would find a way to finish what they had started, but his concern was why they would bother. Had Beaver Jackson told them to keep track of him? If so, why?

After talking with Dawn Sanders, and letting her make a pin cushion out of him, Tony drove to a downtown park along the Deschutes River to let Panzer run and take care of business, and then he proceeded to a frame shop to pick up a bunch of photos he was having matted and framed for his gallery opening. While there, he dropped off the roll of film he had taken at the fried Humphrey house. He didn't expect to find anything in those shots, but he did hope the shot of the security guards turned out. He needed something for his website. Something that praised retroactive abortions.

The photo shop had done a great job on his photos. He worked in black and white, mostly landscapes, but this showing was made up almost entirely of people. Faces from around the world. There was something magical about the human face and what it can tell the informed observer at that vital moment of shutter release. Maybe his skill with a camera gave him a better understanding of human nature. His sister Maria, a professor of psychology at the University of Oregon, had disagreed with Tony's self assessment, and had diagnosed his understanding of others as a direct result of his encounters with thousands of people from all walks of life in more than 30 countries—in and out of the Navy. Okay. . .maybe.

He dropped off the last of the framed photos at the Cascade Gallery a block away. The owner, June Van Hoover, looked them over critically. She was in her early sixties, and if she was five feet then Tony was ready to play in the NBA. So thin was she, he imagined a good breeze would blow her halfway across the high desert to Idaho.

She adjusted her bifocals on a particularly stark photo of a Malaysian woman on the streets of Singapore. One of Tony's favorites.

"I want this one," she said.

That was more words than he'd heard her say in two previous meetings in person. He had called from Eugene prior to coming to Central Oregon, setting up the showing with June's assistant. In person, June had rarely said a thing, preferring instead to grunt and clear her throat.

He left her to admire number two of twenty, Malaysian Woman, while Tony headed back to the condo to regroup. Playing an insurance investigator had taken its toll on him. He needed a shower.

As he was toweling off, his cell phone rang.

"Yeah."

There was nobody on the line. Then he heard breathing.

"Mr. Caruso?"

It was Cliff Humphrey.

"Yes. What can I do for you, Mr. Humphrey?"

"I just wanted to know how the day went," he said. "What you found out."

When Tony took on cases like this, he tried to assess the type of person he would be working for, and if the person seemed like high maintenance, he would usually pass. Life was too short to put up with assholes. Humphrey had intrigued him, though. Tony was usually open to anything after that. Now he was questioning his own judgment.

"I made a few inquiries," Tony said. "Talked with his business partner, neighbors, friends."

"What do you think?"

What he thought and what he knew for a fact were two separate things. "Do you know of anything going on with Dan's work that would have made him...less than happy?"

Cliff Humphrey thought for a while, his breathing uneasy. Finally, he said, "Not really. There was an offer for their company on the table, from what I was told. Some large software company in California had been there a week before his death. It sounded like a good deal to me."

Interesting. "His partner didn't mention that."

"Doesn't surprise me," he said. "It was still preliminary. I think they wanted to maintain control of their baby. It was my understanding they were going to turn down the offer."

Tony switched gears. "Tell me about your son's insurance company and his policies."

Cliff Humphrey gave him the name of the company, and explained that they would not be paying out on his million dollar policy. Barb and Dan were each other's beneficiary, with the same amount. Cliff was secondary beneficiary on both policies, since Barb had no living relatives. And, of course, Dan's mother, Cliff's wife, had died earlier that year in a freak equine accident.

Tony thanked him for the info, told him he would be in touch, and hung up.

Next he checked his e-mail. There was only one message from Melanie Chadwick reminding him they were on for dinner that night.

He gave her a call and told her he'd meet her at the Riverfront at seven, which gave him just enough time to look up a few things on the web before heading over to meet her.

◆

The Riverfront was a huge complex of condos with an older hotel, a restaurant that resembled a Denny's, and one of those dark bars with live music five nights a week. Mostly jazz. A weathered wooden bridge crossed the Deschutes River, with a path that led guests to a drastically hilly eighteen hole golf course. They had package deals where guests could rent a golf cart for a week and park it right outside their door. They could even drive it to local shops that lined the river adjacent to the Riverfront complex.

Being Saturday night, the restaurant was packed. Luckily, Melanie had a friend who worked there who found them a table.

Melanie was at a table set back in a darker area, with a nice view of a huge tropical fish tank. She had a glass of merlot with only a few sips out of it, and one waiting for Tony. She had changed out of her more businesslike skirt at the open house, to a slinky red thing with spaghetti straps working overtime trying to hold her healthy front in place.

She smiled at him, and he gave her a quick kiss as he took a seat in the half-moon booth next to her.

"You look hot," Tony said.

"I'm freezing."

"You know what I mean."

"You don't look too shabby yourself," she said.

He was wearing a pair of loose-fitting olive drab Dockers, and a black polo shirt that stretched tightly across his chest. He wasn't normally prone to showing off muscles, but he thought the shirt had shrunk a bit in the condo's dryer. Either that, or he was eating too much and not working out enough.

They ordered and ate. She had a pork something or other and Tony had the lamb. After dinner they sat back nursing their third glass of wine.

"How was your acupuncture?" she asked.

"The acupuncture itself was quite relaxing," he said, thinking carefully for the right words. "Dawn is an interesting person."

"She is that."

"Are you really close friends?"

"Not really. I sold her the house. She got a good deal. We go out every now and then for lunch. I go in for a massage and a session once a month."

"She does have magic hands," he said.

She lowered her brows at him. "What exactly did she massage?"

"She was very professional. Although I'm afraid she's seen almost as much of me as you have."

"Really?"

"My gown went one way and I went the other." He took a sip of wine.

"Great. Now she'll want to ask you out."

He almost spit his wine out. "What makes you say that?"

"I know her. She has quite the appetite."

Tony wasn't about to mention the comment Dawn Sanders had made to him when she gave him her card. He had no idea how this relationship was going, having only met Melanie recently. Besides, he wasn't even sure he'd be in Bend that long. He had the condo until late January, so he didn't want to get too close to anyone.

They finished their wine and then headed toward the door.

"Would you like to go to the bar and listen to some Jazz?" Tony asked.

She smiled and nuzzled closer to him. "I thought we could go to my place."

He had a feeling this would happen, which is why he drove separate. He needed to talk with a few people in the Riverfront Bar. See if they knew anything about an Italian guy that hung out there.

"Why don't I meet you there in an hour," Tony said.

"Why so long?"

"I forgot I needed to stop by the condo and check my e-mail. I'm waiting for some info to come in on this case I'm working. Plus, I'll need to let Panzer run before I bring him to your place."

She kissed him quickly on the lips. "All right," she said. "I'll try not to start without you."

He walked her out to her car. After she drove away, he went back inside to the bar. This lying thing was getting way too easy, and he almost hated himself for it.

CHAPTER 9

The Riverfront Bar was just that. The place sat a few feet lower than the adjoining restaurant, with double doors that led to a wooden deck that hung over a tranquil set of rapids in the Deschutes. The deck was used year-around, but since it was colder out now, not many people were willing to go out. So, the inside was standing room only.

Tony let his eyes adjust as he squeezed in at the end of the bar, where a couple in their early forties were working on a microbrew.

The busy bartender flicked his chin at Tony, and he ordered a local India Pale Ale.

"Good choice," the man next to him said, turning slightly toward him to allow the bartender to hand Tony his beer. "Let me get that." He flipped the bartender a five from a stack of bills in front of him, and waved his hand, meaning keep the change.

Tony thanked the guy and took a long drink.

He introduced himself and his wife. They were from San Francisco. Up for the skiing. While he told his life story, Tony was able to scan the room, looking for anyone that fit the description Dawn Sanders had given him of the guy that had gone home with Dan and Barb Humphrey the night they died. But Tony couldn't see anyone that fit. Then he noticed two people he did know. The two rocket scientists who had whacked him with the billy clubs that morning out at Cascade Peaks Estates. And they recognized him, as well.

The guy who had been talking with Tony excused himself to go to the bathroom, so Tony slid into the bar stool next to the guy's wife.

She was a nice looking woman. Almost-real blonde hair to her shoulders. Bright blue eyes that said more in a few seconds than her husband had said with words in five minutes. She wore one of those tight silk shirts that was only that way because her obviously-unreal breasts were a little out of proportion to her shoulders. The surgeons in America were making a helluva living, Tony guessed.

"Steve can be quite the bore," she said, moving closer to Tony and placing her hand on his right thigh.

Tony tried to block her out, but her hand was slowly inching toward pay dirt.

Luckily he got his break. A woman he recognized was making her way through the crowd. Dawn Sanders smiled when she saw him, and then followed that up with a knowing grin when she noticed the woman next to him. Tony waved her over. She looked different without her little round spectacles.

Twisting off the chair toward Dawn, Tony said, "You finally made it." He gave her a big hug. "Save me," he whispered into Dawn's ear. Then he gave her a quick kiss and turned toward the San Francisco woman.

She had her lower lip pouting out.

"Thank your husband for the drink, again," Tony said. "It was nice talking with you."

Dawn and Tony walked out through the crowd. He brought her to the outside deck and they stood for a moment at the rail. The river churned loudly below them, but he couldn't see it in the dark abyss. There was a chill in the air, like it was about to snow.

Raising a glass of red wine, she took a sip and then licked her lips. "Where's Melanie?" she asked.

"Went home."

"You work fast. I heard that about Italians."

"We might work fast, but we always finish the task at hand."
She smiled and widened her eyes at him. "How's your back?"

"I want to apologize for earlier today," he said. "I don't like to
deceive people. Especially good people."

"Right," she said. "That doesn't bother me, though. You're an
interesting man, Mr. Caruso. But isn't Melanie a little too sedate
for you?"

He had to laugh at that. Sedate wasn't even close to describing
Melanie. Yet, when he thought about it, she was probably just
that compared to those who frequented the Humphrey Jacuzzi
parties.

Suddenly, the door opened and the two rent-a-cops plowed out
onto the wooden boards. They trudged to within five feet of them
and stopped, their stances wide and identical. They reminded
Tony of a couple of marines blindly popping into parade rest at a
family picnic.

The one who had clubbed Tony, Goatee, spoke first. "You made
us look like idiots this morning in front of our boss."

"Sorry about that," Tony said. "But I'm afraid I didn't help you
out much in that area."

Dawn giggled.

Goatee twisted his head and lowered his bushy brows at Tony.

"Let's go inside," Dawn said, pulling on Tony's arm. "I'm getting cold."

Now the other guy, Flattop, spoke up. "You go. We need to talk
with him."

She hesitated.

Tony nodded. "Go ahead."

She got to the door and looked back at him, unsure.

"Do you work on Sunday?" Tony asked her.

She stared at him blankly, the door against her shoulder.

"Someone might need a session," he said, nodding his head
toward the two rent-a-cops.

She smiled and went inside. But she didn't go far. Tony could
see her watching from through the window.

There was usually a few ways these things could go, Tony knew. A lot of verbal foreplay, followed by pushing. And then someone takes a swing. Since he already knew how these two moved, he didn't plan on letting them hit him first.

The only advantage he had was that the two of them were high school football types; the offensive line variety. The kind that got all worked up but didn't have the agility to throw a straight punch with any speed. They did have muscles though, and if a wild punch did find its mark, Tony could be in trouble.

Fortunately, while in the Navy and not seeing how many brain cells he could destroy, he spent some spare time while stationed in Japan working on a couple of the ancient physical art forms.

"You wanted to say something?" Tony reminded them.

"Stay away from Cascade Peaks," Flattop said.

"Or?"

"He's not going to take our advice," Goatee said to his partner. "I think he'll need some persuasion."

"Wow!" Tony said. "Three syllables. Impressive."

With that, Flattop wound up for a right roundhouse punch. It was like he was moving in slow motion. Tony simply sidestepped to the left, parried his arm, let him slide by, and punched him in the kidney. He followed that up with a right roundhouse kick to his face. That phrase, "The bigger they are, the harder they fall," is true. Especially when the huge guy crashed into the wooden deck face first.

By now Goatee tried to tackle Tony, lunging at him with his arms spread outward. Tony caught the guy's head in his right hand and hooked his left arm under his right, twisted around, letting his momentum carry him past Tony. He twirled flat onto his back on the hard boards. Then Tony drop kneed him in the gut and sent a palm into his jaw, knocking his head back into the floorboards. It didn't knock him out, but he was dazed and confused. More than normal.

Tony left them there in pain, trying to figure out how one guy much smaller than either one of them could have done so much damage so quickly.

When Tony went back into the bar, Dawn had a smile on her face.

"We could go into business together," she said. "You beat the crap out of them, and then give them my card."

The two of them went to the bar, where Tony bought a beer for him and another glass of wine for Dawn.

"Where'd you learn to do that?" Dawn asked.

"While you were studying traditional Chinese therapeutic techniques, I was learning Chinese and Japanese martial art forms."

"You learned well, grasshopper."

By now Tony saw the two geniuses had recovered enough to help each other through the crowd toward the exit. Blood streaked from the nose of each.

Having been distracted from his original intent for coming to the bar, Tony glanced at the bartender. Business had settled down some. The jazz band started playing a mellow tune; a soprano sax player trying out his best Kenny G. Tony thought he might be sick.

"Do you know the bartender?" Tony asked Dawn.

"Yeah, He's here every time I come in."

"Was he working the night Dan and Barb took the Italian guy home?"

"I think so."

Tony nodded for the bartender, and he came directly to him, cleaning the bar with a wet towel along the way.

He was a tall skinny guy, with scraggly brown hair to his shoulders. His most remarkable feature was a nose that flared out at the end like a pig's snout. That wasn't a compliment.

"What can I get ya?"

"Dawn tells me you were working the night Dan and Barb Humphrey were...died," Tony said, leaving it at that.

The bartender thought for a moment. "Work damn near every night," he said. "Wouldn't surprise me."

He had one of those squeaky voices, like someone had clamped his balls in a vise.

"I understand they left with an Italian guy," Tony said.

He shrugged. "I don't worry about who goes home with who around here. Don't pay no attention."

Funny. Tony hadn't said anything about them taking the guy home.

"You knew Barb and Dan Humphrey," Tony said. It wasn't a question, because he already knew the answer.

"Yeah, I knew 'em."

A man plopped an empty mug onto the bar, and the bartender scooped it up and refilled it. Then he returned.

"About the guy they left with that night," Tony said. "Is he local?"

"Don't think so." He was in deep thought now. "Drinks vodka gimlets. Two filberts."

"That's a helluva memory."

"It's my job."

"I know about Barb and Dan coming in here and picking up play things. I don't really care about anyone but the Italian they left with that night."

The bartender scooped up some dirty glasses and plopped them into soapy water. Tony could see his eyes checking him out from the side.

"Sometime today," Tony said.

He turned quickly and said, "What the hell you want from me? I'm supposed to be a picture on the damn wall. People tell me shit they don't tell their priest. I keep my mouth shut and remember what they drink. That's it."

"Dan and Barb are dead," Tony said. "And there's no such thing as bartender/client confidentiality."

The bartender shook his head.

Dawn reached across the bar and grabbed the guy by the collar. "Tell him what he wants to know, Bradley. Or he'll beat the shit out of you like he did to those two assholes."

He shifted his eyes from her to Tony, looking quite scared.

Maybe even more frightened by her than Tony.

"He's from Portland," the guy said. With that, Dawn let him go.

"Keep going," Tony said.

"He's some hardware rep for a Portland lock company. He stays at the Riverfront every time he comes to town. Comes in here every night to see what he can score. More successful than most."

"When's the last time you saw him?"

"That night."

"You got a name?"

"Frank Peroni."

"Like the beer," Tony said.

"Exactly."

Tony got the name of the lock company from the bartender, and then he and Dawn went out front. He was half expecting to find the two rent-a-cops waiting for him, but they were nowhere to be seen. Tony and Dawn stood out front by his truck.

"Remember what I said at my place earlier today?" Dawn said. "If Melanie ever bores you."

Unexpectedly, the entire truck shook, followed by a whining from the back end.

"What the hell was that?" Dawn asked.

"That's Panzer."

"A tank?"

"You'll have to see him. He's built like one."

"I didn't know you were a dog person, Tony."

"I wasn't. Remind me to tell you the story about how I got my hands on this beast."

She pointed a finger at his chest and said, "I will."

Tony thanked her for her help, got in, and drove off, the fading image of Dawn in his rearview mirror making him wonder if he was going in the right direction. After all, he had only been out with Melanie a few times. Not even close to point of no return, a place he had rarely allowed himself to reach.

CHAPTER 10

Tony had told Melanie he would be at her place in an hour.
It took him an hour and a half.

She lived on one of the buttes on the west side of town in a
large three bedroom place she had acquired, compliments of a
cheating-bastard ex-husband. Her words. He had been a prominent lawyer in town until his proclivity for young flesh, an apparent perk of a criminal ethics class he taught at the local community college, became public knowledge. Irony is a funny thing,
but not to the feminist judge who caught the divorce case.
Melanie's ex-husband moved back to California about a year ago,
his tail firmly between his legs.

Melanie told Tony her house was worth about five hundred
thousand in today's market. It was too big for her and her two
cats, but she kept the place more as a constant reminder of how
not to live life, than for any other reason.

Tony parked the F250 in front of the third garage door, let
Panzer out of the back, and then walked the stone path to the
front door. A light snow was falling, sparkling in the spotlight
that clicked on by his movement.

Panzer found a place among the junipers to relieve himself.

Melanie was waiting at the door for him, having changed into
a pair of jogging shorts that resembled silk men's boxers, and an
aerobics top that left her flat belly open.

"I was beginning to wonder if you were coming," she said.

"That's entirely up to you." He turned and watched his dog run from tree to tree. "You sure it's all right for Panzer to terrorize the neighborhood?"

"He'll be fine. I'd let him in, but, as you know, my cats are de-clawed and never leave the house. They can't really defend them-selves against that monster of yours."

"Panzer? He's still a baby."

"Yeah, well, I think my little girls would be one-bite snacks." Tony yelled for his dog. "Panzer!"

Seconds later the dog sat on the stoop next to him.

"*Schlafen heir*," Tony said, pointing to the ground.

Melanie smiled and escorted Tony inside, closing and locking the door behind him.

"You sure he'll be all right there?" she asked him. "It's snow-ing."

"He'll be fine. Couple hours I'll put him in the truck."

"What were you telling him?"

"Oh, I told him to sleep there. He's bi-lingual, but his first lan-guage is German."

They went into the living room, which was a step down from the foyer. A fake gas fire was blazing, surrounded on both sides and all the way to the vaulted ceiling by smooth river stones. It looked like the same workmanship as that at Barb and Dan's burned out house, without the recent charcoal coating. The over-all affect of the room, which was ultimately important to Melanie, was that of a comfortable room. Brown leather chairs sat on hardwood floors. Large plants softened the boundaries.

Melanie had opened a bottle of California cabernet, and it sat on a marble top coffee table breathing.

She poured two glasses of wine and took a seat on the floor in front of the fire. Tony followed her down there, settling into the Navaho rug and leaning against large tan pillows that resembled the bloated belly of a chamois.

"That thing actually puts out some heat," Tony said, feeling the air in front of the fireplace with his right hand.

She took a sip of wine, glancing over the top of her glass at him. "Any e-mail?" she said.

He hesitated. Stalled longer by taking a long drink of wine. "Listen. I don't want to bullshit you. I wasn't checking my e-mail. I had to go into the Riverfront Bar and ask a few questions. I thought it was best that I left you out of it."

"I guessed that," she said, shifting her body closer to his. "You usually check your e-mail with your laptop from your phone in the truck."

"A real Nancy Drew. Maybe I should take on a partner."

She ran her free hand onto his thigh. "Wouldn't that be a conflict of interest."

"I don't have a problem with that."

Her hand moved up onto his lap.

"Find out anything interesting at the bar?"

He was in one of those positions where he didn't want to say anything offensive. "Not really," he managed to say. "Had a little argument with those two rent-a-cops from Cascade Peaks."

"Is that right?" She finished her wine and set the glass down. She had his top button undone and was working on his zipper now.

"Yeah. I was out on the back deck, when they thought I should have some dental work done."

She gave him a whole lot of freedom, taking his instrument of pleasure in one hand while she ripped his pants down his hips with the other. "You had other ideas," she said, her breathing more determined. Not waiting for an answer, she took as much as she could in her mouth.

Tony lay back onto the pillow and finished his wine.

She came up for air. "What else happened?" She went down again.

"Talked with the bartender."

She lifted her head up to him again. "Was it Bradley? He's such a weasel." Down she went again.

He waited for a while before answering, things getting a bit more intense. Seconds later, she got on top of him and did her best rodeo routine. Tony was the bull doing his best to keep up with her frenetic ride. He couldn't help thinking about what Dawn Sanders had said about Melanie being a little sedate for him. She had gotten that wrong.

A while later they rested with another glass of wine, mesmerized by the flames. Then he thought about Dan Humphrey. Why would he shoot his wife and then set the gas fireplace to explode. What was his motive? Tony knew when it came to relationships it didn't take much to set someone off. Maybe his wife Barb had crossed the line during one of their kinky trysts. But that would have been overkill.

"What are you thinking about?" Melanie asked.

"Barb and Dan. What made him do it?"

She took a long drink of wine. "I think I could have done that to my ex, Bob. Especially after walking in on him with his little nineteen-year-old bimbo."

"He brought her here?"

"In our bed. I was supposed to be at an open house for two hours. So he knew he had the place to himself for that long, maybe longer. Usually I go back to the office after the event and get some paperwork done. Problem was, I got to the place we were going to show that day and it was trashed. The owners thought it was the following weekend. So I had to cancel. I was already pissed off by the time I got home. Then finding them there." Her voice became pained and she turned her head away from him.

Over two years had passed from that day, Tony knew, and it still affected her that way. Maybe he was underestimating the power of passion. Maybe Dan had simply snapped. He put his arm around her.

"I was going to tell you about what I found out from the bartender," Tony said.

She sniffled a little and wiped a tear from her eye. "I'm sorry. What did Bradley say?"

"You know him quite well?"

"A little. About the only good thing I can say about the guy is he never forgets a drink or a face."

"That's good to know. He gave me the name of the guy Barb and Dan picked up that night. I'll check into him in the morning."

"You think he might have been involved with their deaths in some way?"

"I don't know. If nothing else, he was last seen with them two hours before their deaths. I'm guessing they took the guy home, had a little fun, then..." Tony shrugged. He had no idea what might have come next.

He hung out with Melanie for another bottle of wine before they drifted back to her bedroom for the bronc-riding competition. The Bend Rodeo in full swing now.

♦

Sitting in his silver Mercedes a block down the street, Cliff Humphrey listened to a Vivaldi concerto on the CD player, his right hand moving with an invisible conductor's baton. The closer Caruso got, the closer he would be to the truth, he thought. He was certain that this crude man would win out in the end. Why would he want to hire anyone who operated with impeccable tact? Who tiptoed around and handled everyone with kid gloves? He might not like these tactics, but he respected the process and the results. And that, after all, was what this was all about. Results. She was something else, though. He cringed thinking of her in his arms. What they might be doing at this moment. Results. Remember that. Results. He smiled and drove away.

CHAPTER 11

In the morning Tony got up before the sun in the strange bed of the real estate broker, feeling uncertain about a lot of things. During the night the snow had turned to rain, and all that remained was a few damp spots on the road.

On his way back to the condo he took Panzer for a long-over-due run along the Deschutes River. When he got back to the condo he took a shower before checking his e-mail. He had one message from Cliff Humphrey seeing what he'd found out.

Sitting out on the deck drinking a cup of coffee, he watched a rather heavyset man searching for his lost golf ball in the bushes on the fringe of the condo's grassy area. The guy looked around to see if anyone was looking, not bothering to gaze in Tony's direction. Then he threw a ball out into the short fairway. After that he waddled out and took a couple of swings before sending the ball twenty yards farther down the course. At that rate, he'd finish the eighteen holes around Christmas. Now Tony knew why people bought condos on golf courses. It was great entertainment.

Tony went inside and logged onto his computer. He knew there wasn't anything he couldn't find out about a person, once he knew where to look. First, he checked into Dan and Barb Humphrey's finances. Tony would be the first to admit he had an advantage with them, since Cliff had given him their Social Security numbers. Once he had that, the rest was easy.

After that, he did a search for information on Frank Peroni, the man Dan and Barb had picked up at the Riverfront. He got his address in Portland and his telephone number. He also checked into the lock company where Peroni worked. Pulled down their address and a few names to contact.

Now he needed to see Frank Peroni face-to-face. Check out his crap meter on him.

As he was about to leave the condo, his cell phone rang. Reluctantly, he picked up.

"Caruso."

"Hey, it's your favorite uncle."

"No shit? Uncle Carlo?"

"You fuckin' putz. It's Bruno. You're gettin' to be a bigger smartass after forty. You know that?"

"Age will do that to ya? What's up, Uncle Bruno?"

"You comin' home for Christmas?"

Tony hesitated. "I don't know? I'm out here in the middle of fuckin' nowhere. Flyin's a pain in the ass this time of year."

"One more fuckin' excuse and I'll send a couple of my boys out to drive ya back."

Great, that's all he needed. Piss off Uncle Bruno. "I'm sorry, Uncle Bruno. Let me think about it. I'm working this case right now. Seeing if this rich kid killed his supermodel wife, shot himself, and then blew the shit outta his house."

"Jesus Christ, kid. Listen to yourself. How the fuck do ya shoot yourself and then blow your house up?"

Good point. "Well, the sequence of events are not clear. The locals here say it happened that way, with some kind of timer or short fuze, blowing the place all to hell. I'm still working out the details."

Uncle Bruno laughed. "Yeah, the devil's always in the details, Tony. Which is why I want you to come home for Christmas. I'm not gettin' any younger, you know. We need to talk business."

Okay. Now he was not only pulling the age thing, but his avuncular responsibilities. Tony had lost his parents in a boating accident on Lake Superior between his sophomore and junior years of high school. He and his brother and sister had gone to stay with Uncle Bruno and his family for his junior and senior years before heading to the Navy. He owed his uncle, but he knew Uncle Bruno would never say so directly. Tony knew the man had never asked him for anything. He let out a deep sigh. "If I can get this thing figured out by then, I'll try for a road trip. I'm not flying, though. Panzer would rip the shit outta his carton."

"That's a good boy, Tony. Your aunt will mix up a huge batch of ravioli."

"I'm not promising anything, Uncle Bruno. I've gotta finish this case. In fact, I'm on my way to Portland right now. I've got to get going."

"Sure. You take care."

There was a click on the other end, so Tony hung up. He looked at the phone and decided to turn it off, shoving it into his coat pocket.

Portland was a hundred and sixty miles from Bend, with no good way to get there. All the roads were two lanes and crossed the Cascades. On a good day, without snow or rain or geriatric land yachts clogging the roads, it would take a good three hours to make the trip, Tony had heard. With the predicted snow, it would take perhaps five or six hours.

It took Tony seven hours, even in four-wheel-drive, which helped with traction but did nothing for visibility in a blinding snow storm. The real problem came when a man rolled his jacked up bronco, and then a semi turned over trying to avoid that, which blocked the entire road for hours.

When Tony finally got to Portland, it was raining like crazy. Surprise.

Darkness had set in completely as he parked out front of Frank Peroni's house in southwest Portland. It was an older neighborhood five or six blocks from the Willamette River, up the hill a ways with an unfortunate view of Interstate 5. Tony suspected, though, that on the rare clear day Peroni could see Mount Hood, which was some consolation.

He sat in the F250 for a moment, wondering how he wanted to handle Peroni. He had thought about simply calling him from Bend, but he wanted to see his face when he asked his first question. If there was any guilt, he'd know. Faces were his specialty.

There were a few lights on in the one-story house. It was one of those neighborhoods built in the late forties where all the houses looked the same, except for the paint job and landscaping.

As he walked up to the front door, he could tell that Peroni hadn't spent a lot of time with a paint brush or with his green thumb.

He knocked and waited. Luckily, the rain that had been pounding his windshield just moments ago, had slowed some. Tony was only half drenched.

Finally, he heard someone coming, then saw an eye scanning him through the peep hole. Tony smiled.

The door opened a crack and he peeked through at a woman in her late twenties. Her dark hair was disheveled, hanging down over her round brown eyes. She wore a baggy Portland State sweatshirt and jeans with holes in the knees. Her tiny bare toes stuck out from the frayed pants bottom, curling into a gold shag carpet.

"Frank's not here," she said. She had a raspy voice, like a lounge singer in a smoky bar.

Tony laughed. "Maybe I'm looking for you," he said.

"Yeah, right. Who are you, and what the fuck you want?"

"Okay. I'm Tony Caruso. I'm looking for Frank. Is he your husband?"

"He's a bum!"

This was going nowhere fast. "May I come in?"

She gave him a quick look up and down; probably trying to assess any danger. He must have passed, because she opened the door for him and cocked her head to one side, telling him to go into the living room. She locked the door and followed him into the room.

The room was highlighted by a reclining Lazy-boy pointing directly at a big screen T.V. There was a worn couch to the side of that. One of those blooper video shows was on the tube, showing how stupid people can be, and how they'll do just about anything for money.

Tony took a seat on the sofa and she sat in the Lazy-boy, her eyes on the T.V. program. She lit a cigarette.

"Where's Frank, Mrs. Peroni?" he asked.

Her eyes shifted sideways through the smoke at him. "If he owes you money, you won't get it from me."

"That's not it."

She turned her head toward him and let out a cloud of smoke in a tiny stream. "You work for Cascade Lock?"

"Why do you say that?"

"Because you're too good looking for a cop." She smiled for the first time. It was a nice set of teeth. She should have done it more often.

"I'm neither," Tony said. "I'm just looking for Frank. Where is he?"

"I have no idea."

That was the truth. In fact, he had a feeling this woman would give him the straight facts on almost anything he asked her. So he forged ahead. "Is he on the road for Cascade Lock?"

"Nope. They haven't seen him either. They keep calling here asking for him. I keep telling them to fuck off, but some people just don't get it. You know?" Her head was cocked to one side like a confused puppy.

Tony knew what she was talking about. In fact, he was probably one of those people. "When's the last time you saw him?"

She thought about that, bringing her cigarette to a bright orange. "Two and a half weeks ago. Just before going to Bend. He loved going there. I don't know why. A bunch of fuckin' yuppies if you ask me." She swung her arm around, pointing off into nowhere. "Same as those people in the Pearl District. Drive around in their BMWs. Sipping expensive coffee. Living on

those golf courses. It's like a mini-California over there. The only
thing good I can say about the place is it doesn't rain like here."

"He didn't come back from his trip to Bend?"

"Hell no! Haven't you been listening to me?" She lit another
cigarette from her first and then snubbed out the end of the old
one.

"Did you notify the cops?"

She gave him a serious, critical glare, as if she were visualizing
his head exploding. "He said he might be heading down to
Medford for a few days. He does that from time to time. Makes
the rounds. I didn't expect him back right away."

"But you did eventually talk with the Portland police?"

"A lot of good it did," she said. Then she laughed at a video.
They showed the same thing again, a man getting hit in the nuts
by his young son with a baseball bat. Hilarious.

"What'd they say?" Tony asked, even though he was pretty
sure what the answer would be.

"Started asking me about our marriage. Wanted to know if
we'd had a fight. Said he'd probably show up if he wanted to be
found. Useless bastards. That's why we pay taxes. To pay for
idiot mother fuckers like that?"

Tony shrugged. "Is there any reason why he wouldn't come
home?"

"Fuck you!"

Sweetness. "I'm just wondering. What about work? Was everything going all right there?"

"Why are you asking all these questions about Frank?" She had
a truly intrigued expression on her face. "Who do you work for?"

Damn. He thought he'd gotten away with that one. He decided
to play it straight. "I'm looking into the death of a couple in
Bend. Your husband knew them."

"You're a cop?" She looked disappointed.

"No. I'm private."

Her eyes brightened. "And you think Frank had something to
do with the deaths?"

"I don't know what to think," he said. That was the truth.

She sat for a moment, considering what he had just said. She flicked some ashes into a tray on an end table. By now the video blooper show had ended, so she flicked through the channels with the remote. When she couldn't find anything she liked, she turned it off. Then she swiveled the chair toward him.

"Our marriage sucks," she said. She pulled the hair back from her right temple, revealing a three inch scar. "The bastard cut me here. And here." She hoisted her sweatshirt, exposing her bare left breast. It was small and sagged with a half-moon scar by the nipple. "Damn near took my nip off."

"Did you report it?"

She covered herself. "That's why the pricks won't look for Frank. Because I did report it. They were pissed because I wouldn't press charges. Hey, I said our marriage sucks, but Frank has his good points. Biggest cock I've ever had." She smiled wistfully.

They talked for a while longer about what an asshole her husband was, but Tony could tell that she really missed the guy. Sadly enough, she probably loved him too.

He was standing at the door about to leave when something occurred to him. "What about his car?" he asked.

"What about it?"

"Where is it?"

She shrugged. "Probably wherever he is."

She told him it was a brown Ford Taurus, gave him the license plate number, and said it had a long crack in the windshield. Before Tony left she gave him her husband's credit card information and their bank account numbers. She assured him there wasn't much in either. Nothing to steal. She also gave him a picture of Frank. He didn't see any resemblance to himself. Maybe she was hoping he would help her find him.

"I'll try to find him," Tony said. Then he left and hurried through a light drizzle to his truck. Panzer was whining, so he let the dog out for a quick relief.

Back in the truck and driving down the street, he didn't know until two blocks down the road that the white Pontiac Bonneville that pulled out after him was a tail.

CHAPTER 12

Tony never had much of a reason to lose someone tailing him. He could have done something dramatic like in the movies and punched it, flying through Portland's streets like a possessed maniac. Although that looked cool on T.V., he didn't have some production company willing to pay for his F250 after he crashed it through a barrier and into the Willamette River. So he took a more subdued approach.

He just kept an eye on the car, making totally irrational turns, ensuring the car was in fact following him.

It was.

He didn't normally carry a gun unless he was going hunting or target shooting. Since he became a private investigator, most of his jobs involved insurance fraud or missing persons. And the later were usually people who didn't want to be found. Guys like Frank Peroni? Maybe.

Thinking about all the reasons he didn't carry a gun, he wished at this moment he had found a single reason to carry one.

He looked into the rearview mirror. There were two men in the front seat. Not as big as the rent-a-cops. But close.

Driving slowly along residential streets, he thought about what he wanted to do. He had worked in Portland a few times with the police. The last time he was part of a task force seeking a unabomber wannabe ten months ago, just after retiring from the Navy. Instead of hanging out in some tiny cabin in Montana, their man lived in a squalid apartment along the Columbia River in the glide slope of Portland International. Turns out the guy was even more dangerous than the unabomber, because his bomb making techniques were as meticulous as a five-year-old putting together playdoe men. Half of the bombs would have never blown up, and those that did either blew the crap out of helpless mail, or fizzled like wet fireworks.

Tony did make a few contacts while in town for a month tracking the guy down. So he picked up his cell phone and called a Portland Police Bureau captain he had spent some time with, drowning a few microbrews. He reached him at home and told him his current situation.

Driving north toward downtown Portland, Tony kept an eye on the Bonneville behind him.

Ten minutes later he pulled over to the curb in front of the administration building at Portland State University.

He just sat there, glancing at the car that had pulled over behind him, watching the two confused men.

Then Tony saw him. A man walking up the sidewalk, a huge German shepherd at his side. When the guy got alongside the Bonneville, he pulled a gun and aimed it at the head of the man in the passenger seat.

Tony took that as his sign to get out. Cautiously he walked up the sidewalk toward the car. By the time he got to the front of the vehicle, his friend, the police captain, had holstered his gun and was laughing.

Captain Al Degaul, wearing a black Nike sweat suit, reached his hand out as Tony approached. He hadn't changed much. At forty-five, his black hair might have had a little more gray. He could have gained a few pounds, but it was hard to tell in the darkness. They shook hands and then Degaul turned toward the two men in the car.

"Tony," Degaul said. "These are detectives Shabato and Reese." His voice was harsh and gravelly like that of a college football coach. Reminded Tony of his Uncle Bruno.

Now Tony felt like an idiot.

The two detectives, dressed more for a night out on the town than for official police business, got out and they all shook hands. Shabato, the driver, was a good six feet, with droopy black eyes. Reese was a few inches shorter than Shabato. His red hair was pulled back into a ponytail. Tony guessed they were both around thirty.

"Sorry for any misunderstanding, Mr. Caruso," Shabato said. "We were watching Frank Peroni's house when you showed up. At first we thought you might have been him. Then we thought you might have been involved with him."

Degaul moved his hand and his dog sat, its tongue hanging out while it panted heavily. Its nose had a patch of gray giving away its age.

"Tony's worked as an explosives consultant with the Seattle and Portland police," Degaul said. "Worked the PDX bomber case. Before that he was a Navy ordnance officer."

The two men nodded their head with respect. It was pretty much a given within the police community that only a crazy bastard would put himself next to a bomb to de-fuze it. It didn't matter if the cop was the most macho guy on the force, it took someone with balls the size of watermelons to play with bombs. What they didn't realize, though, was that the police had hired Tony to consult based on his military ordnance background. They needed him simply to rule out any bomber that might have been trained by the military.

"Why were you checking out Frank Peroni?" Tony asked.

The detectives glanced at each other and then to Captain Degaul.

"Well?" Degaul said.

Reese spoke up first. "His wife reported him missing a couple weeks ago. We were doing a follow up."

Tony wasn't buying that, and neither was Captain Degaul from the look on his face.

"There's more to it than that," Degaul said. "You wouldn't be showing up on a Sunday evening to follow up."

It was Shabato's turn. He raised his dog-tired eyes and said, "We've had Mrs. Peroni under surveillance since she reported her husband missing. Following up the day after she made her report, we went to Frank Peroni's employer. A lock company. They said Peroni was supposed to go to Bend for a few days and then come back. They tried to contact him there at his hotel, but they couldn't find him. We called the Deschutes County Sheriff's office and had a deputy stop by his room. Nothing."

"What about his car?" Tony asked.

"Can't find it," Reese chimed in.

Captain Degaul looked perplexed. "What his finances tell you?"

"That's the point," Shabato said. "That's why we've been watching his wife. There have been cash advances taken four times in the past two weeks, all from Central Oregon cash machines."

Captain Degaul scratched the stubble on his face. "Let me guess. All from different towns."

"Yes, sir," Reese said. "All of them in tourist locations in the middle of the day."

Tony wasn't sure what this was all about. There had to be more to this than the two detectives were saying.

The captain turned toward Tony. "How in the hell are you involved with all this, Tony?"

Damn. Tony thought he'd gotten away without having to answer that.

"Well?" the captain said.

"I'm looking into a murder suicide that took place in Bend two weeks ago."

"Heard about that," Degaul said. "You think Frank Peroni was involved with that?"

"I don't know." That was the honest truth. "He knew the two victims." He was calling them victims now, without even knowing for sure if it was true, at least in the case of Dan Humphrey.

"Yeah, but you've got a hunch, right?" Degaul said. Well he didn't make captain by being stupid.

The two detectives were waiting impatiently for Tony to answer.

"Yeah. Dan and Barb Humphrey supposedly picked Frank Peroni up at the Riverfront Bar in Bend, took him back to their house, and Dan watched while Frank and Barb got it on."

The two detectives smiled identically.

Captain Degaul raised his brows. "Kinky shit. Then what happened?"

"This is all speculation, since Dan and Barb are dead," Tony said. "But the local cops say Dan shot his wife, Barb, and then set his gas fireplace to blow. The house blew up real good. Damn near burned to the ground. Left Dan and Barb looking like Kenny Rogers chicken."

"Who hired you?" the captain asked.

"Can't say."

"Someone who thinks some nefarious shit is going on other than murder suicide," Degaul said.

Tony shrugged.

They talked for a few more minutes. Then the two detectives handed Tony their cards, saying he should contact them if he found out anything else about Frank Peroni. The cops were holding back information. But what? And why? Probably just not trusting Tony.

When the detectives were gone, Tony stood out in the damp night air, gazing toward the city lights. There was something about the sparkle of city lights after a drenching rain. It was as if a layer of slime had been stripped away, making the city somehow more pure. If that were the case, Portland had too many layers, because it rained there a lot.

Captain Degaul asked him over to his place for a beer. How could he refuse that?

CHAPTER 13

They sat up late drinking beer and talking about the case they had worked together. Al Degaul had lost his wife to breast cancer right around the time they were working together on the crazy PDX bomber case. So for the past ten months he had lived only with memories and his fifteen-year-old German shepherd, Rex. His German Sheppard had been his partner on a K-9 unit, and, as is often the case, the dog had lost a step or two and was forced to retire.

Sounded like the story of Tony's life.

Their dogs got along without a hitch, sleeping next to each other near the fireplace.

Tony slept on the sofa and woke with a tremendous headache and dry mouth. After he brewed up a pot of Sumatran coffee, Degaul finally dragged himself out of bed. Rex got up immediately and lumbered to the captain's side.

"Jesus Christ," Degaul said. "What the hell time is it?"

Tony was flipping sizzling bacon by now, about to throw some eggs into the pan. Without checking his watch, he said, "Little after eight."

"Ah, damn!" Degaul picked up the phone and punched in a number. He mumbled a few things and then hung up.

"Someone going to miss the good captain on a Monday morning?"

"You'd think not," he said. "But I got this new lieutenant work-

ing for me. Don't want to send the wrong message coming in late.
She's a real...she's efficient."

"She? Anything I should know?"

He shot Tony a critical glare and then poured himself a cup of
coffee. "Strictly professional."

Tony poured some mixed eggs into the pan, and they instantly
solidified outward. "You been seeing anyone?"

"What the hell are you, my mother?" Degaul took a seat at the
table and sipped his coffee. "Whoa...that's some strong shit."

"You know if you don't use it, it gets smaller," Tony said.

He laughed. "Then I'm gonna have a hard time finding it to
take a piss."

Fluffing the eggs into a perfect stack, Tony flipped them one
last time before plopping them onto two plates. Then he added
three pieces of bacon each. What the hell. You have to die of
something, Tony thought. Besides, he only ate eggs once or twice
a month.

They both ate without saying a word. When they were done and
working on another cup of coffee, Tony noticed his friend staring
at him.

"What?"

"You'll make someone a fine wife some day," he said.

"Fuck you!"

Degaul left a few scraps of bacon and eggs on his plate and
then set it on the floor to his right, where Rex had waited patiently. The dog delicately lapped it up.

Tony's dog sat quietly across the room, not even considering
what the captain's dog had just done.

Having slept really well, thanks to the vast quantity of beer, one
question kept nagging at Tony ever since he woke up. Why in the
hell were the two detectives really so interested in Frank Peroni?

"There's something more to Frank Peroni you can't tell me,"
Tony said.

Captain Degaul hesitated. "Is that a question?"

"Reese and Shabato. Are they good cops?"

"What are you gettin' at?"

"Nothing," Tony said. He felt like he was interrogating his friend. "What I mean is, why are they so interested in a two-week old missing person? Doesn't sound like something you'd put two detectives on, considering Frank Peroni's relationship with his wife."

The captain sipped his coffee, stalling. "First of all, Tony, those two don't work for me. I'm in charge of special units. Secondly, it's none of your fucking business."

"Hey."

"I'm sorry, Tony." He leaned back in his chair, his eyes wandering around the room. "I honestly don't know what they're up to. You're right, though. There's something more to Frank Peroni than the fact that he's missing. That I am sure of."

Tony thanked Al Degaul for his beer, sofa and breakfast, as well as the info. He told him he'd be in touch and gave him his cell phone number and e-mail address.

Then Tony drove west to Beaverton.

It was past nine o'clock, the traffic having died down somewhat on Highway 26 and the surface roads.

Pulling into a business complex, with brick and glass structures no more than three or four stories high, he parked in an unmarked spot and sat for a moment.

He had the laptop on, so he checked the address for Cascade Lock one more time. It was a useless reaction, because there was a big sign out front with the company name engraved in granite. That said something about a company, Tony thought. If a company throws up a wooden sign with the name painted on it, the logical assumption is the company won't be there long. Marble or granite, though, and that shows permanence. This company was here twenty years ago, and still would be in a hundred years. He was sure of that.

Tony went inside. The lobby and reception area on the third floor, where the sign on the first floor said the marketing director's office was, reminded Tony of one of those influential law firms with a hundred lawyers working for Microsoft. Marble walls. Columns. Stone floors. Again, permanence.

An older woman, who still tried her best to look young, sat at an oak desk, a phone notched between her ear and shoulder as she flipped through an appointment book. She was dressed top to bottom in gray wool. Under her blazer was a white satin blouse.

Tony stood patiently waiting for her to get off the phone, gazing at the water colors on the wall. Someone had studied the French impressionists. Finally the woman hung up.

"May I help you, sir?" she said. Her voice had a Tootsie quality, only perhaps a bit more masculine than Dustin Hoffman.

"Yes. I'm Tony Caruso. Here to see Mr. James Burton."

She checked her appointment book, even though Tony was sure she knew he wasn't on it.

"Mr. Burton has an appointment in ten minutes," she said.

He thought quickly. "What about Frank Peroni?"

Her eyes shot up at him. Surprised. That's what he'd hoped for.

James Burton's office was probably as impressive as the reception area. Would have been, if Burton hadn't covered his desk and credenza with mounds of papers that must have taken a small forest to produce.

Burton himself was a tall, stout man in his mid-forties. His remaining hair was a blond gray mix, slicked back, trying to cover bare spots. He wore a fine domestic suit with enough material to make two suits of normal size. His tiny round spectacles could have been a matching pair of the ones Dawn Sanders wore.

Burton stood and shook Tony's hand. Firm. Businesslike.

Tony took a seat in a leather chair that seemed to invite him to stay there forever.

He told the lock man he was a private investigator representing a credit company looking for Frank Peroni. It was as good a lie as any.

"I'm afraid Frank no longer works for us," Burton said, adjusting his glasses even though they didn't need it.

Tony pulled out a small notebook, flipped through a few pages, and stopped on a page where he had scribbled a few notes. It was really his grocery list from when he had first gotten to the condo in Bend.

"Says here he's an account representative," Tony said, using the fancy term for a lock and hardware salesman.

"Was, Mr. Caruso. As I've said, he's no longer with us."

Tony turned a page in his notebook and shook his head. "You wouldn't happen to know where I can find him?"

The man shook his head and his jowls stopped shaking a few seconds after his chin.

"We sent him to Bend over two weeks ago," Burton said. "He never came back."

This conversation was taking a dive in a hurry. But Tony had had a little time to think about what would concern two Portland detectives in a simple missing person, that could have been merely a man who didn't want to be found. So he bluffed.

"Something else is missing from the company besides Frank Peroni," Tony said. Accused actually.

Burton's reaction was incredible. Would have gotten a D in high school drama for that performance.

"I don't know what you mean," Burton said.

Bullshit! That's what Tony wanted to say. Instead, he said, "You know what I'm talking about."

Burton hoisted his body up and rolled toward the door. He opened the door and turned toward Tony. "Our conversation is over, Mr. Caruso."

Tony got up and headed out, but stopped right in front of Burton, his finger pointing at the guy's sternum. "You want to get what's yours, you should have talked with me."

Tony took off and went to the elevator. When he got to the first floor, the doors opened and his two favorite detectives, Reese and Shabato, were waiting, their jaws somewhat slack.

"I warmed him up for you," Tony said, passing them.

Not bad. He'd managed to get thrown out of two offices in just a few days. Unfortunately, that wasn't a record for him.

CHAPTER 14

Tony got back to Bend in the late afternoon. The pass around Mount Hood had been cleared, with the exception of the very top, which still had piles of heavy snow unplowed.

Bend itself was clear and cloud-free, like it was nearly three hundred days a year.

Tony would be the first to admit that his methods when working a case were somewhat unorthodox. Trying to use logic, he collected information from those he thought should give him what he needed to know. Then he sifted out the bullshit. What remained should be the truth. Problem was, damn near everything he was currently collecting seemed to be irrelevant bullshit.

He didn't know if Frank Peroni had anything to do with Dan and Barb Humphrey dying, yet he was certain the man knew something about it. And the fact that he had disappeared right around the same time as their deaths was reason for concern. He'd watched far too many old episodes of Barnaby Jones to dismiss the notion that Frank might have died in the fire at Cascade Peaks Estates. Since there hadn't been much left of Dan after the blast and blaze, it was a possibility.

Tony pulled into the parking lot of a new development west of Bend's old downtown. It was one of those trendy complexes of tourist shops, condos, and high tech manufacturing along the Deschutes River on the former site of a huge wood products facility. At one time a couple thousand people used to work there during Bend's heyday as a lumbering town. Pickup trucks and black coffee. Now it was Beemers and cappuccino.

As he walked up to the building housing Cliff Humphrey's development company, he stopped for a moment taking in the scene of Mount Bachelor to the west. He had found out that this was Humphrey's second office. The main office was in downtown Portland on the twentieth floor of the Lange Building, a tall mirrored generic structure with a view of Riverfront Park and the Willamette River, and, presumably, Mount Hood whenever it wasn't raining.

Looking out across the Deschutes, Tony realized that almost directly across the river was Dan Humphrey's old office. Dad looking down on son. Nice.

The outside of the building was stone over wood. It was a single story structure with a prime spot along the river. Canada geese wandered about in the wet grass along the shore.

Inside was a large, open room with fairly modest industrial carpet, pure white walls with original watercolors, and large plants positioned nearly everywhere. There were a few drafting desks facing away from the bank of windows that ran the length of the room. Tony could see why. The architects wouldn't have gotten any work done with a view of the Cascades like that. In the center of the room was a few more desks divided by padded partitions.

There wasn't much activity in the place for a Monday. Maybe the boss had let them go early to catch some of the powder that had fallen on the mountain the night before.

A receptionist sat at the front of the large room. Although she had all the attributes of a full-fledged woman, she looked prepubescent in her retro 70s attire. Reminded Tony of someone he might have asked to a high school dance in the Disco era. She was wearing one of those headset phones over curly red hair, talking at someone who didn't want to listen. So she hung up and smiled at Tony.

"You're Tony Caruso," she said.

"Good guess."

"It wasn't a guess," she said. "I looked you up on the web for Mr. Humphrey. Saw the picture of you after that explosion in Seattle."

One of his finer moments. Tony had damn near lost his left arm in that debacle. He had been shadowing a young bomb squad officer who had watched one too many Mel Gibson movies where the crazy cop tries to decide if it's the red wire or the green wire to cut. Tony was right in the middle of telling the rookie not to try to outguess a bomber, who could be colorblind anyway, and try to figure out where the wires were going. Too late. Luckily it was only a small charge pipe bomb.

"That was my right side," Tony said. "My left side is better." He cocked his head to the side for her to see.

She laughed.

Cliff Humphrey came out of his office, startled when he saw Tony, and then came over and shook his hand.

"Let's talk in my office," he said, and then escorted Tony away from the reception area.

Humphrey's office was decorated in a southwest motif. Navaho rugs. A carved wood sculpture of an eagle. Tall cacti in two corners by the windows.

Cliff Humphrey took a seat in his plush brown leather chair that squeaked with the slightest move he made.

Tony's chair was leather also. In fact, it could have been cut from the same steer as the one in Larry Gibson's office across the river.

"What have you dug up, Tony?" Humphrey said. He had his hands on the shiny oak desk in front of him, his fingers rolling nervously.

"Do you know a man named Frank Peroni?" Tony asked.

His fingers stopped. "No. Should I?"

Tony laughed at that. "How am I supposed to know what you should know?"

Humphrey gazed off at the river and then rose from his chair.

"It's a nice day. Let's go for a walk by the river."

Tony wasn't sure where that came from, but he didn't argue. He was always game for outdoors over indoors.

They walked down to the river. Geese waddled away from them as they approached the water. The walk from the building had given Tony time to think. Somehow Cliff Humphrey knew Frank Peroni. He was sure of it.

"You see this complex," Humphrey said, spreading his arms out like Moses parting the Red Sea. "I conceptualized the whole thing. Came up with the idea of condos and shops side by side, along with the new industry. There are bike trails that follow the river to downtown. Buses come right through here picking up residents for Mount Bachelor. You could walk to work here, walk downtown for dinner, and even shop for almost anything you need right here."

Sounds nice, but why was he telling Tony this? He wasn't sure.

"People think that developers are Lucifer in the flesh," he said. "They think we'll do anything to make a buck."

Okay. Now Tony had to speak. "Seems to be some truth to that."

Humphrey tried to laugh. "Maybe so. In fact, I know some people in Portland who might think of me that way. But it's just not true. We opened our Bend office almost fifteen years ago. There was huge potential here. Californians had discovered the place. Moved here in droves, selling their houses in L.A. and San Francisco for big bucks and then building veritable mansions on golf courses or up on Awbrey Butte for a fraction of what it would have cost them back home. We have people at Cascade Peaks who moved here from Singapore and Hong Kong. The influx has slowed somewhat in the past few years, but that won't last long."

"Is that why you want to build the new destination resort up the mountain toward The Three Sisters?"

Humphrey looked surprised. "You've heard about that?"

Tony nodded. Anyone in Bend for more than a day would have had to be brain dead to not hear about that.

They started walking upstream toward the park used in the summer for open-air concerts. There was nobody there today.

"It may never happen," he said. "Still has to clear the county land use board. They're not sure Bend needs another resort."

"I also heard the property is land-locked. It would cost a lot if everyone had to fly in to their houses."

Humphrey thought about that for a moment, as if he were actually considering the concept. "We'll get the land," he assured Tony. "We always do."

Tony had a feeling he did. He started to walk away and then stopped, his eyes locked on Humphrey's uncertain expression. "I stayed at a nice condo unit near Yachets recently," he said. "They've got a week in September available for five grand. Is that a good price?"

Humphrey shrugged. "It's a steal. I know the guy who built that place. A week was fifteen grand a few years back. I'll give him a call and have him hold it for you. You can check out the unit after you prove Dan didn't do this."

His words came out almost like a warning to Tony. Find in his way or else. "Listen," Tony said, "I'm sure it must be very difficult for you. With your wife's death this year. . ."

His expression filled with incertitude, Humphrey said, "You do your homework."

"I like to know who I work for."

Humphrey turned toward the northeast and lifted his chin as he said, "She died over near Prineville on a ranch. She was an excellent rider. Dressage. Western. Won enough ribbons and trophies to fill a huge mahogany case I had built for her." His eyes seemed to tear up and his throat clamped down.

"I'm sorry," Tony said. "I shouldn't have brought it up."

After some hesitation, Humphrey turned to Tony and said, "Don't find yourself alone, Tony. Find a good woman and have children. This is painful, but you have to remember all the good times. This will pass with time. That's why you have to find out the truth, Tony." His watery eyes indicated nothing less.

◆

Cliff Humphrey had just returned to his office and barely sat down when a side door opened and a woman dressed in Bend business attire, a white silk blouse, dress slacks, and cowboy boots, stepped in and took a seat across from him, her left leg tapping on the Navaho rug.

"What he find out?" Melanie Chadwick asked, her teeth biting down on her lower lip.

"Wanted to know about Frank Peroni," Humphrey said.

"Where'd that come from?"

He shrugged. "Portland, I guess. He didn't tell you why he was going there?"

She wrinkled her nose and said, "Hell, no. We've only known each other for a couple of days. What's the problem? You always knew Peroni might pop up in his investigation."

Humphrey sunk into his leather chair, his expression wavering from concern to indifference. He shook his head. "This is getting out of hand. Maybe I should call the whole thing off. Pull Caruso from the case."

Melanie's foot stopped tapping and she rose suddenly, her hands on her hips. "Bullshit! This development will go through. That's the plan. Stick with the plan."

Humphrey tried to calm her with open hands lowering toward the seat. "Take it easy, Mel." He smiled and let out a slight laugh. "I lost my son, here. Not to mention my daughter-in-law and possible grandchildren. My whole legacy is lost." With those words he rose and went to Melanie, placing a hand on each shoulder.

"Don't, Cliff."

He turned and went to the window, glancing down at the river. This had to work, he thought. Or all of it would be for nothing. He couldn't let that happen.

CHAPTER 15

One of the problems with being single at Tony's age was that it was easy to forget that someone else might be interested where he might have been for the past couple of days. He wasn't entirely sure he wanted to concern himself with such trivial aspects of life. He was either dead or alive, he figured, and someone would eventually find out which were true, unless he ended up face down in the high desert with buzzards picking at his decaying ass.

In Tony's case, under his current situation, he had called Melanie from his cell phone just after crossing the pass on his way back from Portland. She had sounded relieved, but tried to hide it with humor. She'd offered to have him over for dinner. She was going to make a curry stir fry.

Tony got to her place around six p.m. He was worn out slightly from the drive and from racking his brain over this case. He knew where he wanted to go as the crow flew, but navigating the narrow roads below was frustrating.

She gave him a kiss on the cheek as he entered.

"The news said the snow was really bad on the passes yesterday," she said. "Lots of accidents."

He took a seat at the kitchen counter. Steam seeped out of a large pan on the stove, bringing the smell of ginger, curry and soy with it. "It took me seven hours to get to Portland. Some idiot flew past me and then crashed a few miles up the road."

She poured him a glass of Chianti and handed it to him.

"What were you up to in Portland?"

"Checking into the guy who went home with Dan and Barb the night they died."

She nodded, went to the stove, and lifted the cover on two pans. Then she dished up fried rice and chicken curry stir fry. They sat at the counter to eat, neither saying a word for a few minutes.

"Sold a house today," she finally said.

"Big one?"

"Four hundred thousand."

"That'll be a nice commission."

They finished eating and Tony excused myself to go to the bathroom. On the way back through the master suite, he sat on the bed to use the phone. He needed to check his messages. As he was listening to his messages, he noticed a small piece of paper on the nightstand with a number on it. He almost dismissed it, but the number looked familiar. When the last message went through, he pulled out the card Cliff Humphrey had given him. The number on Melanie's nightstand was Cliff's cell phone number.

As he was getting up from the bed to leave, he turned to find Melanie standing in the doorway.

She stared at him blankly. "What's up?"

"I was just checking my messages," Tony said, pulling his cell phone from his pocket. "Battery's dead. By the way, I'd love to come to dinner." He tried on a smile.

"You should check those more often." She turned and left him there.

Tony was a little confused and tired, so he decided to get the hell out of there. He had a feeling she wanted an after dinner treat, but he wasn't sure that was a good idea.

Driving back to the condo where he was staying, his mind wandered. On one count he should have asked Melanie why she had Cliff Humphrey's cell phone number on her nightstand. More reasonably, though, it was none of his business. He was so preoccupied, he didn't notice anything out of the ordinary as he pulled up to the garage. At least not until the door wouldn't open with the remote.

"Fuck!"

Tony got out in the darkness, leaving his truck door open, the headlights shining his way, and went to the door, giving it a tug. Knowing anything about electric garage doors, which Tony did, he should have known that was a total waste of time. Even the Incredible Hulk couldn't yank the door through an electric motor. But he pulled on it anyway, just for the hell of it. Damn near ripped his arm out of the socket in the process.

He wasn't sure what made him turn back toward the truck when he did. Maybe he heard a rustling in the bushes. Maybe he had some sixth sense telling him to turn. Maybe he was the luckiest bastard in Oregon. Whatever it was, he turned just in time so the first bullet merely grazed the front of his shoulder. If he hadn't turned it would have probably severed his spine, or at least lodged itself into it, since, based on the pop, it was a small caliber round.

But the flash and crack of the bullet in the night air gave him enough time to dive behind the front of his truck as the second and third rounds smashed into the garage door.

Again, Tony wished he had a gun. Two times in two days. But even if he did have a gun, it wouldn't have helped him much in this situation, except maybe to scare off the shooter.

He crouched behind the front of the truck waiting, imagining whoever had shot the gun was watching his headlights for his shadow. He scanned the outer pines along the visitor parking area, the direction from which he had seen the muzzle flashes. Nothing.

Then he heard it. A vehicle starting up and tires screeching.

He got to his cab and turned off his lights. Then he checked the back of his truck. Panzer was quiet and that bothered him.

"You all right, boy?" Tony asked, after lifting the topper door.

Panzer greeted him with a lick to his face.

"I'll take that as a yes."

It took the first Deschutes County sheriff's deputy less than five minutes to get to the condominium complex. Not a bad response time. Must have passed the shooter along the road leading down from the golf community, Tony thought.

In fifteen minutes, there were four cars surrounding Tony's area, their lights circling around the roofs. People from some of the other condos were out on their balconies gazing about, wondering what in the hell was going on.

Tony had wanted to avoid talking with the local cops until the time was right. Now he had no choice.

The first young deputy on the scene, not knowing the story, pulled his gun on Tony. He raised his left arm, since his right was in some pain from the bullet ripping flesh. When Tony said he had been shot, the deputy finally approached him cautiously and let him put his arm down.

Tony was keeping his mouth shut until someone with authority showed up. No use explaining himself more than once.

Finally, a man approached wearing blue jeans and a Blazers sweatshirt. He had just been talking with the first man on the scene. He was a tall beefy guy, his hair almost completely gray. He had a Hitler-like mustache, the only type military personnel or cops were allowed to have, and which Tony had always found amusing. But the man's most significant physical feature was his tremendous head. It gave him the impression of a bear that had been feeding at a nuclear waste dump.

"I'm Sheriff Bill Green," he said, shaking Tony's left hand.

Tony told him his name, nothing more. He figured if he told everyone he was a private investigator, how private could that be?

"What happened here?" The sheriff looked directly at Tony's shoulder. "Is that all right?"

Tony looked at the blood, which had soaked into the sleeve of his Columbia jacket. "It hurts, but I'll live."

He was still waiting for Tony to tell his story.

"I was set up," Tony said. He told him what happened with the door. How he got out to try to budge it. How he was standing right in his headlights. The only thing he didn't tell the cop, was that he felt like an idiot.

"Why would someone want to shoot you, Mr. Caruso?" the sheriff asked.

"I don't know. I'm basically a nice guy."

He smiled. "These things are normally domestic," he said. "Are you seeing anyone in town?"

Tony hesitated. "Melanie Chadwick."

His brows shot up. "I know Melanie. She sold me my house. She's a great woman."

He was beginning to think that everyone in town had bought their home from Melanie.

The sheriff continued, "She went through a nasty divorce. I'll have my people check to see if that asshole of an ex-husband is back in town. Could you believe someone wanting to cheat on her." The cop shook his head side to side.

Tony wanted to tell the sheriff he was pretty sure Melanie's ex had nothing to do with it, but he decided to let him go off in that direction. Keep him busy.

An EMT came over and placed a bandage on Tony's right shoulder. It wasn't much of a wound. He'd probably bled more when he fell off his bike as a ten-year-old. The problem was it was a ripping cut through the flesh and would need six or seven stitches or he'd end up tearing it open every time he shifted his truck.

So the good sheriff ended up driving him to the emergency room. He had no intention of climbing into the back of an ambulance rig with that puny little scratch.

CHAPTER 16

On the ride to the hospital, Sheriff Green started with the questions again. He had a relaxed form of inquiry that was worth examining. It was like sitting down with the family priest and talking about the meaning of life, without the possibility of forbidden sex. Tony almost wanted to answer each question truthfully. If he hadn't been on guard he might have actually done that.

"What do you do for a living, Mr. Caruso?"

"I'm semi-retired," Tony said. It wasn't a total lie, since he was collecting a Navy pension.

"Military?"

"How'd you guess?"

"I'm a detective." He hesitated, while he navigated a sharp curve on the winding road down the mountain. "You walk with confidence. Thirty-one inch stride. You're still relatively young. And corporate America doesn't give many pensions these days. You wouldn't have said semi-retired if you weren't making some money from that retirement."

They came to a stop sign and then continued on toward downtown Bend.

Tony hadn't realized he'd given so much away with a simple phrase and his walk. But he was right. Anyone with any knowledge of the military could recognize another who had been there. Especially if the person had been any good at it.

"I'm guessing you were a Marine," Tony said. It would have been a compliment for anyone but an Army soldier.

"Long time ago," he said. "Recon." He let the word hang in the air as if Tony should bow down to some unseen God.

They were in downtown Bend now, stopped at a light. There were two young men in their early twenties, wearing their best snowboarder grunge, walking in the crosswalk in front of them.

"Take those two," the sheriff said. "There's no discipline there. They couldn't find their ass with both hands. A couple of lost souls."

Tony glanced at them, thinking they were probably millionaire partners who owned some computer software firm. A little farther to the west and south and they would have qualified for surfer dudes. But Bend had no surf, with the exception of ski slopes with snow boarders, and those were as plentiful as sagebrush.

They took off and wound through relatively quiet streets toward the hospital on the east side of town.

"Which service were you in?" he asked.

"Navy."

He smiled, and Tony guessed it had something to do with the rivalry between sailors and marines.

"Ordnance," Tony added.

That took the smile away. He glanced at Tony sideways. "You were one of those crazy bastards?"

"Afraid so."

"When I was doing a little work in Southeast Asia, we came across some unexploded ordnance that our own Air Force had dropped. Anti-personnel mines. Needless to say, we stayed clear and called in the ordnance folks. Those silly bastards walked right down the field scooping up and defuzing the mines like they were picking daisies." He shook his head. "They didn't pay those guys enough."

Tony was feeling kind of queasy, and it had nothing to do with his bullet wound, which he was sure had stopped bleeding long ago. He thought about the explosion on the tug that had taken part of his hearing and the life of his best friend.

"You didn't say what else you do, Mr. Caruso. Besides being semi-retired."

He'd only been working as a private investigator in Oregon for a year now, but he'd already found a good way to describe what he did without actually saying it.

"Sometimes people hire me to look into things," Tony said.

"Private detective," the sheriff said, filling in the blanks.

They pulled in front of the emergency room door and there was a man in scrubs with a stethoscope wrapped around his neck waiting for them. Sheriff Green parked in a restricted zone and shut off the engine.

"Maybe this shooting has something to do with what you're looking into now," the sheriff said.

Tony started to get out, but stopped. "I didn't say I was currently looking into anything. Maybe I'm just here for the great skiing."

They got out and the sheriff followed Tony into the emergency room, where the nurse set Tony on an exam table behind a curtain and started asking him the normal questions. Pertinent things. Like if he had insurance. Then he actually took Tony's vitals.

When the nurse went away for a moment, the sheriff, sitting on a rolling metal chair, scooted closer to Tony.

"Why don't we cut the bullshit cat and mouse, Mr. Caruso, and you tell me what you're working on."

Tony still had a few more people to talk with before he started asking him about Barb and Dan Humphrey. But he didn't want to totally piss him off either, or he'd get nothing when he really needed it. So he decided he really needed a friend in high places in Central Oregon. Not just for this case, but for any future cases.

"All right..." Tony was cut off by the doctor coming in and kicking the sheriff out of his chair.

They gave him a tetanus shot in the arm, cleaned out the wound, and then twelve stitches, followed by a fancy new bandage. When the medical people were done with him, they told him to come back in ten days so they could remove the stitches. He agreed and started to leave.

The sheriff said he'd give Tony a ride back to the condo. They took a different route back. Longer than normal, Tony realized.

Once they started getting close to the golf community, the sheriff let out a heavy sigh. "You were going to tell me what you're working on," he reminded Tony.

The delay had given Tony time to construct how much he wanted to tell the sheriff. "Do you ever take on a case even though you know it's totally useless? A complete waste of time?"

The sheriff shrugged. "Maybe."

"You might do it just to make someone feel good," Tony said.

"What are you getting at?"

"I'm looking into the death of Dan and Barb Humphrey."

"But—"

"I know," Tony said. "Dan shot his wife and then killed himself. That's what I keep telling the insurance people."

"You're working as an insurance investigator?"

If he said yes he'd be lying to an official peace officer, which if it wasn't illegal, was at least unethical. "Let's just say I'm asking a few questions." There. It wasn't a lie. In fact, he'd given the sheriff enough to realize who had probably hired him, considering how vocal Cliff Humphrey had been with the sheriff and the media.

Stopping at the gate for the golf community, the sheriff powered down the window and waited for a young security guard to get off the phone. Finally the guy came to the sheriff's door.

"Yes, sir," the guard said. "What can I do for you, sheriff?"

"Did one of my guys ask you if you saw a car speed away from here just before they arrived following the shooting?" the sheriff asked.

"Yes, sir. Deputy Harris. I told him that I was on the phone talking with my boss when the car flew through. At least I think it was a car."

"So you didn't see it?"

"No, sir. Afraid not."

"Thanks," Sheriff Green said.

They pulled away and a minute later settled into the condo parking lot alongside Tony's truck. Panzer was still in the back. Tony got out and started to close the door.

"Just a minute," Sheriff Green said.

Tony leaned back inside.

"You be careful," he said. "You play around a rose bush, you're bound to get poked."

Not sure if the good sheriff was talking about his current case or Melanie, Tony closed the door and the sheriff backed out and pulled away.

As he walked toward his truck, which was still not inside the garage, he thought for a minute about who he'd pissed off enough to make them want to shoot him, and he was coming up with a blank. Certainly not the two rent-a-cops. Or, as the sheriff had suggested, Melanie's ex-husband. The only thing to do in a situation like this was to keep plugging away. And hope they didn't succeed in plugging him.

He opened the back of his truck and Panzer jumped out onto the pavement. The dog immediately ran toward the berm where the shooter had taken the shots, his black body moving back and forth among the manzanita and low junipers.

By the time Tony reached Panzer, he had stopped, his nose concentrating on a spot of grass.

"Good work, Panzer." Tony stooped down and gave his dog a hug with his left arm.

CHAPTER 17

In the morning, Tony got up and took a shower, trying his best to keep the bandage on his right arm dry. His shoulder was sore, and the area around the wound swollen like he'd been stung by a bee the size of a bald eagle.

Standing naked in front of the mirror, he twisted around to look at his back. The bruises where the rent-a-cop had hit him with his stick were in the yellow-green stage. They didn't hurt much any more, unless he poked a finger right into them.

He got dressed and went into the living room.

His dog greeted him, his tiny tail wagging so hard his entire rear end nearly rose from the hardwood floor.

"All right, Panzer," he said, his left hand working a special spot behind the schnauzer's ears. "Go out and take a good dump. But not on the green. That's just too much of a hazard for those duffers."

The dog headed for the door and waited.

Once that deed was completed and Panzer had gotten some running out of his system and now lay on his pad near the sliding glass door, Tony sat down and logged onto the computer to check his e-mail. Nothing but a few junk e-mails. Then he went onto the web and searched a few companies.

He started with the Portland company where Frank Peroni worked. The lock company was third in sales behind Schlage and

Sergeant, but moving up the list fairly fast. The headquarters was in Beaverton, with regional offices in Denver, Des Moines, and Raleigh. Each region had reps like Frank Peroni that covered a couple states out west and maybe a single state in the more populous east. Peroni, although he worked out of the headquarters, was actually a western regional rep covering Oregon and Idaho.

Next he checked into the software company out of Palo Alto, California. The one that had made a bid on Dan Humphrey's company. For Tony, looking at their earnings and capitalization was like trying to understand the tax code. Something he had no real desire to learn. He did understand the stock market enough to know that brokers had high praise for the company, buying up damn near every available share and making heavy profits each quarter over the past few years. Much of this money had been made because of the company's heavy involvement with internet financing software and their encryption technology. They were so successful, in fact, it made Tony wonder why the company wanted to buy a small firm from Bend.

His last stop on the web he looked into the Bend software firm, owned exclusively now by one Larry Gibson. Nice earnings. Gradual growth until the last year when they went from six employees to twenty-five and moved from downtown Bend to their new facility along the river. Interesting.

Tony finally had a direction he wanted to go.

As he left the condo, Panzer at his side, he did what he normally never did. He looked at the name of the lock on his door. It was a Cascade Lock.

He got outside and wandered toward the garage. He was more cautious than he had been the night before.

The air was still crisp from the clear sky, not a cloud anywhere. It was supposed to reach close to sixty.

Pulling the truck out, he stopped and turned off the engine. Then he got out and walked up the landscaped berm to where he guessed the shooter had stood. Gazing back, and considering the angle, distance, and the lighting the night before, he was amazed he was still standing. He should have been dead, or at least strapped in a wheel chair drinking dinner from a straw. The area had been thoroughly trampled by the sheriff's deputies. They had found three spent .22 long rifle brass casings. Virtually impossible to trace, considering damn near everyone and his brother and sister in Deschutes County owned a .22.

He got back into his truck and headed toward town.

Tony went directly to the county court house. He was always amazed at the kind of information he could find skimming through county records. Public officials nationally might have been puffing their chests proclaiming a need to streamline government, but the bureaucracy, in its most negative interpretation, was alive and well on the local level. A damn permit was needed for everything except becoming a parent, and Tony was sure that was coming soon.

First he checked into Dan and Barb Humphrey. Found their marriage license, their tax records for their home, and Dan's application, with Larry Gibson, for a business license. There was no record of an impending divorce, which didn't mean a thing.

While he was there, he checked into Cliff Humphrey's land use permit for his destination resort. Going back farther, he found where Cliff Humphrey and a group known only as HGE Enterprises had purchased over five hundred acres of rough land. What about listing agent? He flipped through to the next page. There it was in black and white. Three Sisters Realty. Listing agent: Melanie Chadwick. Now he knew why she might have had Cliff Humphrey's cell phone number.

The Deschutes County Sheriff's office was in the building next to the court house. Tony walked over and stood out in the hallway for a moment, wondering what he wanted to say to the sheriff. It was closing in on noon.

A busy secretary the size of a Sumo wrestler filed paperwork in the top shelf of a metal cabinet. She wore a dress that could have been the tent for a boy scout patrol. Colorful flowers bursting for freedom. She was stretched out on her tip-toes, her leather sandals about to burst from fat, stubby toes.

When she finally turned to Tony, he was surprised, because her face didn't match the rest of her body. She had dark hair and eyes like that of an anorexic model.

"May I help you?" she asked pleasantly.

"Tony Caruso. Here to see the sheriff."

She checked the clock on the wall.

"He's probably on his way to Jerry's Cafe down on Wall Street," she said. "Eats lunch there every day. Then he walks back along the river to his office." She laughed gutturally. "Thinks he can burn off his lunch with that little walk."

He thanked her and left, checking his truck tires to see if some meter Nazi had marked it with chalk. Nothing. He looked in the back and saw Panzer sleeping on Tony's bed, instead of his own pad to the side. Figured.

Then he walked the four blocks to Jerry's Cafe.

Jerry's was an anachronism for Bend's trendy cappuccino and pesto bagel new age image. As Tony walked in and looked around, he could have been in Topeka, Kansas in 1975. And the place wasn't made up to look that way. It had simply gone from 70s modern, survived the 80s and 90s without change, and made it to a place so retro, it had been discovered again in the new millennium.

The place was filling up fast with the lunch crowd. Professionals in casual suits next to students in baggy jeans.

The sheriff was in a corner booth with red vinyl seats, sipping a cup of normal coffee, and reading a copy of the local daily newspaper.

When he saw Tony approach, the sheriff smiled and nodded for Tony to take a seat across from him.

"How you feeling?" the sheriff asked.

"Like someone shot me in the arm."

A waitress came by wearing an actual frilly apron. Tony turned his cup over and she filled it without saying a word, before continuing on down the line of booths and tables.

"Nothing extraordinary about the lead we pulled out of the garage door," Sheriff Green said. "Just your normal .22 long rifle. Not your normal choice if you want to kill someone."

Not for an amateur, Tony thought. But if he wanted to kill someone without making too much noise, that's what he'd use. It's almost impossible to trace. And if you hit the guy in the head, the bullet will enter but not exit, bouncing around inside the head like a Ping-Pong ball and making scrambling eggs of the brain. If the victim didn't die, they'd wish they had.

The sheriff continued. "Maybe someone just wants to get your attention."

"I'm listening," Tony said. "Problem is, I don't know who I've pissed off this time."

The sheriff laughed and then took a sip of coffee. "So you rub people the wrong way sometimes?"

Tony shrugged. "Doesn't everyone?"

"Not to the point of being shot at."

"Right."

"You got something on your mind there, Tony? You don't mind if I call you Tony?" the sheriff said.

"Tony is fine."

"What's on your mind?"

"I just came from the court house," he said. "Doing a little research. What do you know about Cliff Humphrey and the destination resort he wants to build west of town?"

Before the sheriff could answer, the waitress brought him a huge club sandwich cut in triangles and held together with toothpicks. She asked if Tony was going to order and he said no, just the coffee.

"You mind if I eat while I talk?" the sheriff said.

"Go for it."

Sheriff Green picked up a triangle and shoved a good portion of it into his mouth. When he was almost done chewing, he said, "That's who you're working for?"

Tony didn't say a word or show him anything non-verbally.

Maybe that was a mistake.

"Humphrey might have a little problem this time around," the sheriff said. "Might have bit off more than he can chew." He laughed and a piece of bread flew out his mouth onto the table. "I should talk."

"You don't think the county will issue him a land use permit?"

He shook his head. He'd just taken another bite and his mouth was really full now. When he finally had it down his throat, he said, "Don't see how they can. He still hasn't gained access and I don't think the water board will approve it."

"Why not?"

"Have you seen the plans?"

"No."

"The amount of water they'd require is too great for our twenty-year plan. That's a lot of green space to keep green. A long distance to pump it up hill, too. That's not to mention the hold out denying him right of way. Although he may have softened some after that robbery on his place a few weeks back."

"Robbery?"

"Yeah," the sheriff put a small chunk of sandwich into his mouth, chewed on it with one side while he spoke out the other. "Damn near took everything he owned. Someone pulled a moving van right up to the front door. He's not the only one. We've been having a rash of them lately. Driving me nuts. Real professional job. No breaking. Just entering."

Now that got Tony thinking. Maybe Cliff Humphrey was playing hardball with one of the last obstacles to his resort.

"Who's the holdout?"

"Don Sanders."

"The acupuncturist?"

"No, D.O.N." the sheriff said. "It's her brother."

Now he knew this town was smaller than he had thought. He left the sheriff to finish off his sandwich and newspaper.

CHAPTER 18

It was nearly one o'clock by the time Tony got back to his truck to get Panzer and then walk the four blocks from downtown Bend to Dawn Sanders' acupuncture clinic. The weather was nice. Not a cloud in the sky. The forecaster had been right. It was close to sixty.

Telling Panzer to sit and wait, Tony walked right into the clinic this time through a screen door without knocking.

A young woman with straight blonde hair to her waist stood behind a small glass-front counter that contained herbal remedies, Chinese serenity balls and tea.

"Nice dog," she said.

"Thanks," Tony said, glancing toward the door.

"I have an Australian Shepard. You don't see many Giant Schnauzers. Mostly the mini variety."

"You're absolutely correct. Most people think I either gave him growth hormone as a pup, or he grew up next to a toxic waste dump."

She giggled. "You're that Italian guy Dawn told me about."

"Guilty. Is she in?"

"Afraid not. It was just too nice out. She brought her lunch down to the river. You can catch her there."

"Thanks," Tony said on his way to the door. He stopped and said, "I'd like to see that Aussie of yours someday."

Laughing again, she said, "And I'd like to show you."

"Ciao."

Once outside, he whisked his dog away from the clinic toward the river.

When he got down to the Deschutes River, he found Dawn feeding the last of her sandwich to a gaggle of geese. She was wearing long spandex pants with running shoes, and an oversized maroon sweatshirt with the sleeves shoved up to her elbows. She didn't see him until he stopped a few feet from her.

She turned, and with surprise said, "Tony. Are you looking for me? Or is this just some cosmic coincidence?"

He smiled. "Your receptionist said I could find you here."

She gazed at the geese. "I know I shouldn't do it," she said. "They should have flown south by now. But everyone fattens them with bread, so they don't want to leave. Many stay all winter now."

He didn't say anything.

"How's your shoulder?" she said.

He glanced down at his right arm. "Is nothing sacred in this town?"

"They broadcast that stuff over open frequencies," she said. "But I have friends at the hospital. We don't get many shootings around here. Except for domestics."

"Like Dan and Barb Humphrey?"

She hesitated. "Yeah."

They started walking along the river toward the foot bridge that crossed into an older westside neighborhood. Panzer ran around the groomed edge of the river, keeping his distance from the geese. The dog had learned his lesson in Seattle a while back, getting a peck on the nose.

"Who would want to shoot you, Tony?" she asked.

"I don't know."

"You have something you want to ask me," she said. "I can tell."

"Are you a psychic as well as an acupuncturist and a massage therapist?"

She stopped and looked at him seriously. "Actually, yes. To a certain degree. I have feelings, but they're not very clear. For instance, last night I was sitting around the house and felt a strange chill. I had an intuition that something bad was about to happen. Then this morning I find out that you were shot. Weird, ha?"

He wasn't a real skeptic when it came to the sixth sense. If the experts were correct, and people only used a tenth of their brain, then it stood to reason that some people might actually be able to use another part of it for more than cranial filling.

"You didn't happen to see who pulled the trigger?"

Unexpectedly, she put her arm through his, like they were high school sweethearts, and pulled him along toward the bridge. They went out onto the middle of the wooden walking bridge, leaned against the rails, and gazed back at Mirror Pond, an elongated part of the river that slowly passed Bend's downtown and reflected the city lights at night.

Tony had a feeling about Dawn Sanders, thinking that somehow they would become friends, if not more. She was the kind of person who enjoyed each breath she took, savoring the moment. It was as if tomorrow was never certain, so don't waste today.

"Well? What are you trying to tell me?" she asked.

"I was wondering about your brother, Don."

She narrowed her brows, confused. "What about him?"

"I hear he's the only thing standing in Cliff Humphrey's way to building his destination resort."

She turned away from him and gazed down into the water flowing by. "Don won't budge on that."

"You think Humphrey had anything to do with Don's house getting broken into?"

She turned back quickly. "That's what I told Don. But he wasn't sure."

"Did Don ever go to any of Dan and Barb's wild Jacuzzi parties?"

She laughed so hard Tony thought she'd fall off the bridge.

When she finally settled down, she said, "You've never met my brother, have you?"

"No."

"Go talk to Don," she said. "He's working down in one of the southeast subdivisions. Paulina Ridge. I'm sure he'll be happy to talk with you."

He wasn't sure if she was being sarcastic or not. But he agreed. As he was about to leave, he thought of one more thing.

"How close are you with Melanie?" Tony asked.

She shrugged. "Not at all."

"Do you know if she knows Cliff Humphrey?"

She laughed again. "You're kidding, right? You don't know much about her, do you?"

"I guess not."

"Her and Cliff were an item a while back. Right after she and her husband got a divorce. She didn't tell you?"

He didn't have an answer for her. But now things were starting to make a little more sense.

Dawn put her hand on his. "Why don't you come to dinner tonight," she said.

He mulled it over. "Let me give it some thought."

Suddenly, Panzer came flying up and stopped a few feet away.

"What an interesting dog," she said, looking around. "I wonder whose it is?"

"Panzer, *sitzen!*"

The dog responded and sat onto the wooden planks.

"This is your dog?" she asked, stooping down for a better look. "The one from the back of your truck the other night?"

"Yep."

Looking up to him, she said, "May I pet him?"

"Sure."

She put a hand behind each ear and gently stroked Panzer's favorite spot. The dog's eyes closed and Tony thought about his own experience with those hands recently. Dawn seemed to know where to touch.

"What kind of dog is he?" she asked. "He looks like a big ol' schnauzer."

"He's a Giant Schnauzer."

"I've only seen the miniature type."

"There are three types; miniature, standard and giant."

"You spoke German to him. Is that where you got him?"

"Yeah. My last assignment as a Naval officer was a three-year exchange with the German military. Just before I left they gave me Panzer as a gift for my work there."

She suddenly stopped petting his dog and rose up to Tony. "You were a Navy officer?"

"Is that a problem?"

"No. It's kinda sexy. Like *An Officer and a Gentleman* sexy. What were you doing in Germany?"

"Mostly drinking beer." He hesitated, looking deep into her eyes. "When I wasn't working on my master's degree in international relations, I was training the German Air Force and Navy on a few new weapon systems that we were selling them. I was assigned at the installation where they train their military working dogs. Shepherds, Rottweillers, Dobermans, and Schnauzers. Panzer's parents were both bomb dogs. In fact, his military pedigree goes back a hundred years. Don't ask him about the Nazi years, though."

"Why did they give him up?"

"I was introduced to him and he immediately took to me. The Germans weed out those dogs that are not strictly business."

"He didn't have the nose for it?"

"Just the opposite. He's a little over two years old now, but before they gave him to me at just under a year old, Panzer was introduced to nearly every explosive compound in existence. He never forgets. Giant Schnauzers have been bread for their intelligence, endurance and their exquisite nose."

She reached down and rubbed Panzer behind the ears again. "Well I just know he's a sweetheart."

A breeze came up and Panzer lifted his nose into the air.

"I better get going," Tony said. "Your brother is at Paulina Ridge?"

"Yeah, you can't miss it." She gave him directions and then said, "Think about dinner."

He headed off toward his truck, Panzer running side to side in front of him.

It took Tony fifteen minutes to get to the Paulina Ridge subdivision. He had a lot running through his head, but not enough to realize that his arm wasn't hurting. Pulsating under the bandage, the wound felt like it was going to suddenly blow up.

Paulina Ridge was one of those places where the houses sat behind a stone wall, but not quite exclusive enough for a gate or a security guard. There was only one phase of fifteen or so houses completed, with perhaps half of those occupied. Workers in bulldozers were clearing and leveling an area to the south, with another crew scampering about farther down from them.

Tony parked his truck and stepped down into the dirt. A man came running toward him waving his arms. He was a dirty, scruffy-looking guy with a ZZ Top beard. He had a yellow hard hat on, and his hair frizzed out from the brim, making him look like Bozo on acid.

"What the fuck you doin' here, Dude?" he yelled, getting way too close for Tony's comfort. "Can't you see we're about to blow the shit outta some lava rock?"

He spit a nice wad of tobacco, just missing Tony's new Nike cross trainers.

Tony looked around, trying to find a warning sign or anything else to indicate this was a blasting zone. Zilch. Once he looked more carefully, he noticed some wires stretched out to three separate sites that lead to a box maybe ten feet in front of his truck.

"I think you should mark this a little better," Tony told him.

"Listen, shitforbrains," he said. "The sales office is up the hill a ways. Go talk to Zelda up there if you wanna buy a place."

"I'm not here to buy," Tony said. "I'm looking for Don Sanders."

The man checked him out more carefully now. "What da fuck ya want with him?"

"I'm a friend of his sister, Dawn."

He really considered him this time. "You aren't that Italian guy, are ya?" He paid particular attention to the 'I' in Tony's nationality.

"Afraid so."

"Well I'm Don Sanders." He held out his grimy right paw, which was missing the pinky. They shook and pain shot up Tony's arm tempting to pop his stitches. "What ya need? By the way, you really should be more careful in a blasting zone. Coulda got your ass blown up. My sister wouldn'ta liked that."

Without saying another word, Don Sanders went over to the control device, waved his arms at two other men standing off a ways from the explosives, glanced back at Tony momentarily, and then set the charge.

If Tony hadn't been familiar with explosives and watching things blow up, he might have been alarmed by the shaking ground and the lava rock and dirt flying high into the air, not to mention the tremendous noise. In fact, he even had enough time to cover his good ear. He looked back at his truck, hoping the topper had cut some of the sound from reaching Panzer.

When the dust settled, Tony followed Don Sanders toward the blast site.

They stood over a covered hole of broken lava and gnarled wood from juniper roots.

"Cool," Don Sanders said.

Sanders gave his two men instructions on what needed to be done next, and then Don and Tony wandered under a large ponderosa pine.

Sanders pulled out a can of chew, shoved a wad into his right cheek the size of a golf ball, offered Tony some, but Tony declined with a shake of his head. Tony had tried chewing tobacco once in high school right before a baseball game in his sophomore year. Threw up twice, once just after sliding into second base off a double. Vowed never to try the stuff again.

"So, what ya got on your mind?" Sanders said, his tongue working the tobacco into his cheek.

Tony wasn't sure where he was going with this, but that never stopped him in the past. With Don Sanders, anything but the direct approach would be sniffed out as bullshit.

"Tell me about your land squabble with Cliff Humphrey," Tony said. Couldn't get any more direct than that.

Sanders' eyes shifted and he spit a straight stream of brown cud into the dusty ground. "Not much to tell. That dipshit wants my land. I don't want him to have it."

That was straight enough on his part. "Isn't he offering you a fair price?" Tony asked.

"You work for that bastard?"

Tony hesitated. Maybe too long. "I'm just asking a simple question. I could care less if the man builds a destination resort in Bend." That was the truth, and Don Sanders seemed to sense it, Tony could tell.

Sanders ran his grimy fingers through his beard. "The only reason I'm even talking with you is because my sister told me about you. If she likes you, I guess ya gotta be all right." He thought for a breath or two before spitting. "The price isn't the problem. I probably would have sold out to the guy until my place was ripped off. Don't like those kind of tactics." He shifted his eyes about as if they were being observed or listened to by some unseen enemy.

"What's the problem?" Tony asked.

"He's a powerful man."

"Cliff Humphrey?"

He nodded his head yes.

"You think he ripped you off?"

"Damn straight! That ain't all. I'm lucky to have any work in this town. The bastard blacklisted my company. Only reason I got this gig is because I went to high school with the developer. He was the running back and I was the pulling guard. Saved his ass many times." He smiled and his teeth were brown with tobacco.

"There's got to be a lot of lava rock to blast out for a development the size Humphrey is proposing. Couldn't you work out a contract for that, plus a fair price for your property?"

Sanders thought it over, as if he hadn't considered that before. "I don't know. I don't like the idea of working for him. Are you sure you don't work for the guy?"

"That's not my agenda," Tony said, which was really the truth.

"That's what Dawn told me," he said, and then hocked up a nice wad and sprayed it airborne through his teeth. "Said you were looking into Dan and Barb's deaths. Thought that was figured out."

Perfect opening. "There's still a few insurance issues open. I'm just trying to confirm what the authorities have called it. You knew Dan and Barb?"

He shuffled his boots in the dirt. "Not good. They were the microbrew and espresso type, and I'm more the cold Bud and burnt black coffee kinda guy."

"You know them enough to have an opinion on their death?"

He shrugged. "Opinions are like assholes. Everyone's got one."

Tony waited.

Finally Sanders said, "I don't know. They seemed about as happy as most couples these days."

That wasn't exactly an encouraging indictment. "You think Dan could have killed her?"

Sanders spit and then said, "I think anyone's capable of murder depending on the circumstances."

Tony didn't want to piss someone off who had access to explosives, but he couldn't help himself. "Where were you the night Dan and Barb were fried like Smores at a boy scout campout?"

Sanders narrowed his intense eyes on Tony and said, "Fuckin' my mare up the ass."

"Great," Tony mumbled.

Without saying another word to him, Don Sanders ran off yelling and waving his arms at one of his men. Tony wandered back to his truck. Just before getting in, he noticed something on the ground. He stooped down and picked up the one-inch piece of wire. It was the same color, could have been from the same roll and lot, as the piece he had found at the base of Dan and Barb's burned out fireplace.

He gazed down the hill at Don Sanders, and his long beard seemed to wave in the breeze back at him again, telling Tony to go screw himself.

CHAPTER 19

It was late afternoon by the time Tony got back to his condo.
He got himself a beer and took a seat at the small table in
front of the sliding glass door. Cracking the door open slightly, he
glanced out at the golf course. There was no one to be seen anywhere, since the temperature had dropped some and low clouds
had moved in off the Cascades.

Something was bugging him about the development Cliff
Humphrey and his partners wanted to build. According to
Melanie, the housing market in the area had started to slump a little, with the high-end houses taking the biggest hit. So why build
now? What did Cliff Humphrey know?

He got up and went for his second beer, retrieving his laptop
computer on his way back and hitching it up to the phone. When
Tony took on a case, one of the first things he did was check into
the person who hired him. In this case, since the guy was a friend
of his Navy friend, Joe Pellagreno, he hadn't done a thorough job
of checking out Cliff Humphrey. That could have been a mistake.
Maybe Tony figured the guy's reputation should stand for something. Maybe he didn't think the case would bring him anywhere
the local cops had not already been. Whatever the reason, he had-
n't done his normal complete background check.

Pulling up Humphrey's development company, Tony sifted
through the normal crap, and, seeing he was getting nowhere,
decided on another direction. At the court house he had found out

HGE Enterprises was the company trying to get land use for the new destination resort. So he checked into that company. Bingo! Under the principal owners were Cliff Humphrey and James Ellison.

He finished his beer and headed out.

By the time he got to Cascade Peaks Estates, all that remained of the sun was a pink hue behind dark swirling clouds in front of Mount Bachelor and the Three Sisters. He pulled the truck over in front of the burned out house and sat. His eyes weren't focused on the fried shell that used to be Dan and Barb Humphrey's place. Instead, he gazed directly at the home that resembled a Scottish hunting estate. The home of Mr. and Mrs. James Ellison.

His mind drifted off, thinking about how the two rent-a-cops had jacked him up out front, the conversation he had had with the captain, Beaver Jackson, and then the talk with Mrs. Ellison.

Starting the truck, he drove up into the driveway. When he got out, blinding lights flicked on, startling him for a moment. He continued on and knocked at the front door.

Mrs. Ellison peered out from a side window at him, gave a strained smile, and then opened the door for him. She was wearing a tight aerobics outfit with sweat visible at various spots.

"Mr. Caruso," she said. "What brings you by?"

"May I come in? I have a few more questions."

She hesitated long enough for him to sense the answer would be no, but then relented, opening the door for him.

Tony stepped inside and glanced around, looking for a sign that her husband might be there. He could hear a Puccini opera sifting in delicately from the other room.

"Would you like a drink?" she asked. She had a bottle of French water and took a quick gulp from it now.

"No, thanks. I was wondering if I could talk with your husband, James?"

She considered that carefully, her eyes inspecting him. "I'm afraid James is away again. San Francisco."

There was silence for a moment while he tried to think of

something to say. He wasn't sure how much she knew about her husband's business.

"What can you tell me about HGE Enterprises?" Tony asked her.

She seemed to expect the question. She shrugged. "Not much. My husband is one of the principal investors. He finds ways to infuse capital into projects."

Deliberately, she drifted toward the room the music came from, and Tony followed her, trying his best to keep his eyes off her swaying hips. They went into a library with mahogany book shelves that lined two walls on either side of a stone fireplace. She took a seat in a large leather chair, hoisted her right leg un-ladylike over an arm much like Frank Peroni's wife had done, and took another sip of water.

He was feeling a little uncomfortable. Unsure where his questions would lead. Unsure what questions to ask.

She nodded her head toward an identical chair across from her, and Tony took that as a sign to sit, so he did.

"Gianni Schicchi," Tony said in his best Italian. "O mio babbino caro."

She looked surprised. "Mr. Caruso. I had no idea you were an opera fan."

"It's not something you bring up very often," Tony admitted. "But when you grow up in an Italian family...with a name like mine."

She shifted her left leg out. "Any relation to Enrico Caruso?"

"He was a distant cousin." Tony did his best to keep his eyes from centering on the area between her legs, which was hard considering her presentation.

As she adjusted the thin strip of aerobics suit between her legs, her eyes narrowed directly toward his. "What do you want?"

"Excuse me?"

"What do you want? Really?"

He was confused by the question. Especially since her hand was still sliding over the mound between her legs.

"HGE Enterprises," he managed to get out. "I was just wondering...how your husband was involved with that." This was partially true. He knew what venture capitalists did, but he actually wanted to know how her husband and Cliff Humphrey had gotten together, without coming out and saying it.

She slid her hand up and flipped the left strap to her suit off her shoulder, giving her left breast nearly enough freedom to roam about. "HGE Enterprises," she said formally. "James founded the company with Cliff Humphrey when they started Cascade Peaks." She suddenly got up and headed toward the foyer, stopped at the door and turned her head toward him. "Let's talk out here." Then she disappeared around the corner.

He was sitting there feeling like an idiot. So he got up and followed her. It wasn't too hard to find out where she'd gone. He simply followed the trail of discarded clothing out to the deck, catching a glimpse of her naked body as she lowered herself into the Jacuzzi. Tony reasoned that if he had a wife who looked like that, he probably wouldn't leave town as often as her husband did.

He stood a few feet from the Jacuzzi trying not to be too obvious with his eyes. But she was sitting just high enough for her nipples to protrude like periscopes from the churning water.

"You wanna join me?" she asked him, her southern accent escaping more than ever.

"I just took a soak this morning."

"I'm sure you could do it more than once a day," she said, her eyes drifting down his body midway. "I don't guess you'd have a shriveling problem."

He'd probably hate himself later for this. "I should probably get going. I'll show myself out."

She stood up, exposing herself fully. "Are you sure," she said, disappointed, her hands on her hips.

He let out a deep breath. "No. Yeah. Have a great evening."

She sunk back into the water. "It coulda been so much better," she said in her best whiny debutante.

Tony headed toward the door, his gait somewhat affected by shifting blood flow.

When he got back out to his truck, he sat for a moment gazing at the Ellison residence. Standing in the second floor window, elegantly naked and appealing, was a dark silhouette leaning against the frame.

Reluctantly moving his eyes to his right, he glared at the burned out Humphrey house, thinking about what had happened there and how life was rushing forward all around. He recalled the two spots where bodies had fallen to the carpet. What was the point? If Dan shot his wife and then himself, why blow the house all to hell? That bothered him more than anything. And he hated unanswered questions.

Tony backed out and started to drive away, but then farther down the road the house where the basketball player lived caught his attention.

For the first time there were lights on. So he pulled in to athlete's driveway and parked.

CHAPTER 20

Tony must have rang the door bell twenty times before the large oak door swung open. He was expecting to see some huge man that he'd have to look up to. Instead, there was a young black man, early twenties, who might have gone six-two in his high-top Nikes. He was wearing a pair of baggy black shorts to his knees. That's all. The Blazers had done a fine job with him in the weight room. But he was also wearing one more thing. A brace on his left ankle. His large round eyes inspected Tony as if he were one of his coaches about to reprimand him for a stupid mistake.

"What's up?" he said. "I didn't order no pizza."

Tony wasn't sure if that was a cut at his heritage. "That's good. Because I don't have one."

The basketball player started to close the door and Tony caught it with his foot and hand simultaneously. "Are you Jamal Banks?"

He let out a breath. "Who da fuck are you? You want my autograph or something?"

Tony didn't want to deflate the guy and say he had no idea who he was or how good he could put the round ball through the ten-foot hoop, so he simply smiled and said, "Not exactly. I was hoping we could talk about your neighbors." Tony nodded his head toward the Humphrey house.

"Never met 'em," he said. "Hey, listen...I'm not suppose to

stand on this ankle. I'm in rehab."

"I just need a few minutes," Tony said. "May I come in?"

He considered Tony carefully now and then glanced behind him. "I'm trying to find a little pussy," he said, showing Tony his perfect teeth. "Are you some cop?"

He got that a lot. "Some kind," Tony said, hoping it would open the door farther.

"Motherfucker," he said, drifting away from the door. He hobbled into the living room area and took a seat.

Tony was somewhat surprised when he got into the room. There were plants all over the place. All the chairs and sofa were quality leather set onto shiny hardwood floors. The music was Seal, barely loud enough to hear. Tony stood quietly glancing about the room.

Suddenly, a young blonde woman came from a back room. "I can't find that cat anywhere, Jamal." She stopped when she saw Tony. "Oh, hi. Is this your agent?" she asked Jamal.

She was wearing jeans too baggy and a sweater that gave her upper body the appearance of a llama. She was the receptionist at Larry Gibson's office. Small town indeed, Tony thought.

The basketball player swished his head.

"I can't find that cat," she said. "She was here yesterday...came right out when I came through the door." She looked at Tony again. "I know you, Mr. Caruso. You came by our office the other day."

"Right. How is Larry Gibson?"

She looked confused at the question. "Fine, I'm sure. He doesn't like you much."

"Oh? Why's that?"

"Didn't say." She smiled and headed toward another room. "Here kitty, kitty."

Tony turned to the basketball player, who was looking somewhat disgusted. "Sorry," Tony said. "Now, what can you tell me about Dan and Barb Humphrey?"

"Told you I never met 'em."

"Never saw them mow their lawn? Gardening?"

He laughed. "You fuckin' crazy? These people don't do their own lawn. They have it done by some wetback." His glare centered on Tony, his head cocked to one side. Then he said, "You don't know shit about basketball do you?"

Tony shrugged.

"I was traded to the Blazers this year after spending my rookie season at Golden State. I just bought this place in September. With training camp and flying around the country for games, I've only been here a few times."

"Why'd you get a place here, so far from Portland?"

He shifted in the chair. "I have a condo in Beaverton. My agent worked a deal for this place as part of my Nike contract. It's a great investment."

"So you never met Dan and Barb?"

He hesitated. "Not really. I seen 'em a few times while golfing. They sure did like that hot tub."

The woman came out of the bedroom holding a six-month-old kitten that seemed to blend right in with her sweater. Jamal got up to meet her, and then took the kitten and pressed it against his dark chest, the kitten nuzzling and purring against his bare skin.

"There you are," Jamal said. "Where da hell you been?"

Tony left the two of them there to play with their pussy.

When he got out to his truck, Panzer was on his feet, his nose pressed against the sliding window of the topper.

"What you want?" he asked his dog.

Panzer whined at him and then licked the screen, leaving a nice white film behind.

"You smell something?" Tony looked across the wide green space between the basketball player's yard and the old Humphrey place. "I'll bet you do."

He got in and drove off toward the north side of town. While doing so, he called Dawn and asked for a rain check on dinner. Instead, he grabbed a quick chicken sandwich at Wendy's. Not much of a substitute, he realized.

There was at least one constant in life that Tony was certain about. If he ever needed any information from a desk clerk at a hotel or motel, or even a condo complex, never go there in the afternoon or early evening. That's check in time for most places, and if they were doing that, he might as well take a seat in the lobby and watch Fox News for a while. Early evening was nearly as bad. People were looking for replacement towels, since they'd trashed theirs down at the pool.

No. The best time for information was some time between ten and midnight, any later and the desk help would get nervous.

So, after not finding out much from Mrs. Ellison or the basketball player, Tony made his way across town to the Riverfront Hotel complex.

There was a woman in her late twenties at the desk when he walked in. She wore a brown uniform that fit her round body tightly, showing more rolls than she should have. Her long dark hair was one step away from gale force. She had a pleasant smile for him as he leaned on the desk.

"May I help you?" she asked.

"I hope so," Tony said. "I'm looking for my brother. I understand he's staying here. Or was staying here. I'm really not sure."

She looked confused.

"Let me explain. I'm from Boise. I get a call from my sister-in-law saying she hasn't seen my brother Frankie in a while. He travels to Bend on business and sometimes has to stay longer than expected. But it's been longer than normal."

Tony had a feeling she was buying into his sob story, so he paused for a few seconds, as if trying to control his emotions.

"I can check the computer," she said, "see if he's here. What's his name?"

"Would you? I'd really appreciate it. Frank Peroni."

She clicked away at the computer and stopped suddenly, her eyes uncertain. "This is strange."

Tony leaned forward trying to catch a glimpse of the screen. "What?"

"Says here he never checked out, and..." She clicked at the keys a few more times. "His bill wasn't paid."

"That must be a mistake," Tony said. "My brother never leaves without paying."

Just then a man in his mid-thirties came from a back room. He was a large man with three chins and a gut that hung over his belt. He was a disgrace to any uniform. The kind of guy the sheriff would hate, Tony thought.

"You talking about Frank Peroni?" he said. He was chewing on a huge wad of gum.

The woman nodded. "Yeah. This is his brother."

"You're the second person to ask about him...well, third actually, this evening."

Tony gazed at him, hopeful.

"There were two guys here about a half an hour ago, maybe less."

"What they want Frankie for?" Tony asked.

The guy shrugged. "They were from his company. Said they needed a key to the condo."

"Condo?"

"Yeah, Cascade Lock owns the condo. We just manage it. Normally there'd be no charges involved with Mr. Peroni's stay. But he was here during a black out period, a time set aside for tourists, so he would have had to pay for the time he spent here. He scheduled the place for a week. When he didn't check out, I called the company and they told me to hold it for Mr. Peroni. Didn't want us to rent it until futher notice."

"Why didn't the two men from his company pay for the room charges?" Tony asked.

"I asked if they'd cover the charges," the big guy said. "They said they'd have to run the charges through their finance office."

Tony thought about that. "Why don't you give me a copy of the bill. If the company doesn't pay Frankie's bill, I will. I promise."

The woman looked at the guy, who shrugged. Then she hit print and ran him a copy of the bill.

"Thank you, sir," the guy said. "I wish everyone was that conscientious."

Tony tucked the paper inside his jacket. "The Peroni's pay their bills," he said before turning to leave. When he got to the door he turned and looked the guy directly in the eye. "The guys from his company. Did one of them have long red hair pulled back into a ponytail, and the other guy was a bit taller with droopy eyes?"

"Right!" the guy said. "You know them?"

"Yeah, nice guys. I think they work in human resources." With that Tony smiled and walked out.

He got into his truck and thought for a moment. Portland Detectives Shabato and Reese were a bit out of their jurisdiction. He pulled out Frank Peroni's bill and scanned it for a moment. He wanted it for the dates. But more than that, he wanted a good look at that unit, and the number was right there for him.

He started the truck and headed down the hill toward the condo units.

CHAPTER 21

Private detectives on T.V. approach a door, scan the area for anyone who might be watching, and then within seconds pick their way into some apartment. Tony was sure that could happen. Problem was, he had this terminal respect for privacy. He wouldn't want someone snooping around in his underwear drawer, so why should he suspect someone else would?

All these things flew through his mind as he wandered along the outside hallway to Frank Peroni's condo unit. The outside of the building was rough-cut wood, giving the place a rustic look. The stairs and wooden floor were scuffed from ski boots and golf shoes. He watched the numbers on the doors pass, hoping he wouldn't succumb to some primal instinct and force his way into Peroni's place.

He could see the door ahead and he stopped suddenly when he heard a sound coming from within. A rustling sound. Like someone looking for something. Damn! He leaned over the railing, glancing down to the parking lot, and there it was. The same white Pontiac Bonneville that had tailed him from Frank Peroni's house in Portland. Shabato and Reese.

Tony had to know why those two were so set on finding Peroni. So he inched closer to the door, trying to hear them inside.

They were talking to each other.

"Damn Blazers blew a twenty point lead last night," one of them said. "And to the Clippers. What the hell's that about?"

Tony got next to the door.

"They didn't have that young kid shootin' threes," the other one said.

"Sprained ankle my ass. Probably out smokin' pot."

Tony laughed to himself as he grasped the door knob. He quickly opened the door.

Inside, the two cops, surprised, responded by going for their guns. When they recognized Tony, they shoved their guns back into their holsters.

"Jesus Christ," Reese said, as he flipped his red ponytail over his shoulder.

"What the hell you doin' here?" Shabato said. His droopy eyes blinked at Tony as if he'd just stared at a solar eclipse.

Tony closed the door behind him. "Same as you. Looking for Frank Peroni." He glanced around the room, noticing the two of them had made one hell of a mess for the housekeeping staff. "Only I wasn't planning on breaking into a man's condo and rifling through his shit."

The two of them glanced at each other.

"This is official police business," Reese assured him.

Tony laughed as his eyes shifted from the sofa cushions on the floor, their covers taken off exposing their white spongy innards, to the grill hanging off the air conditioning unit under the front window. "So, then...you'd have an official warrant?"

They hesitated long enough for Tony to realize the stupidity of that question.

Shabato patted his jacket. "Damn. Must have left it in Portland."

"Why don't we just cut the bullshit," Tony said. "You tell me why you're so interested in Frank Peroni, and I'll tell you everything I know." Which wasn't a whole hell of a lot. But they didn't know that.

The cops looked at each other again, as if neither could speak without first consulting the other through some cosmic mind meld.

"You first," Reese said.

Damn. He had a feeling they'd say that. He sat down and explained everything he knew about the man, from him going home with the Humphreys to speculation that he could have been the one fried at their house. He did explain that it was an unlikely supposition on his part, but the possibility did exist. When he was done, the cops simply stared at him.

Reese was the first to speak. "All right. We've been investigating Frank Peroni for six months now. We got a tip from his employer that a shitload of their customers had complained about break-ins. Said their locks weren't worth shit. Blah, blah, blah... So we started looking into it."

"Yeah," Shabato spoke up. "Turns out there's something to the complaints. Peroni sells a high-end product to some of Portland's best developers. People who specialize in million dollar homes."

"Wouldn't they have high-priced security systems?" Tony asked.

Reese took the question. "Usually. But Cascade Lock deals in those as well."

"Let me guess," Tony said. "You think Peroni is ripping these people off. He makes money selling the lock systems, and then he goes and wipes the place out once the people move in."

Reese shook his head strong enough so his ponytail landed in front of his shoulder. "We don't think he ripped them off himself. He has an alibi for every break-in. We do think he gave someone the codes and the keys."

Tony thought about that. One hell of a racket. Make money coming and going. "Why haven't you made an arrest?"

Shabato laughed, his eyes closing to tiny slits. "We had the bastard set up in a sting when he disappeared."

Something just occurred to Tony. The sheriff had told him about a rash of burglaries in the area. "Have you talked to the local sheriff? There've been a lot of burglaries in this area as well. Maybe Peroni's been active here also."

They both considered it. Reese said, "You might have something there."

Tony got up and went to the door, stopped, and turned toward the two of them. "I have no idea if Peroni was involved with the Humphrey..." He wasn't sure what to call it. "Incident. I do think he knows something about it, though. When you two find him, could you give me a call?" Tony handed Reese his card with his cell phone, e-mail and web address on it. Something he rarely gave out.

Reese shrugged. "Sure. If we find him."

With that, Tony left them to continue bringing down the value of the condo. Funny. That's probably what Melanie would be thinking.

CHAPTER 22

It was overcast the next morning. Tony could tell that the mountains were getting a fresh coat of powder, and he would have normally taken that as a sign to go snow shoeing, but he had questions that needed answering. Questions that wouldn't go away. Questions he had been hired to find out, yet had somehow been distracted from. Like whether or not Dan actually killed his wife and then set his house to explode. Basic questions.

He decided to go back to the source. Cliff Humphrey. Tony caught him parking his Mercedes at the office.

"Jesus!" Humphrey said, stepping back a few paces. "You startled me."

Humphrey wore a clone of the suit he had on the night he hired Tony. Same nice fabric, only this one was gray like the sky.

"Sorry to bother you," Tony said. "But I have a few questions."

Looking around, Humphrey seemed unsure if he should go inside. Finally, he said, "Let's go into my office."

They did just that. Humphrey led the way, unlocking the door, since he was the first one to show up. As they passed through the door, Tony couldn't help noticing the lock. Cascade. They went into his office and Tony took a seat and waited for his current employer to do the same.

When Humphrey was comfortably in place behind his desk, Tony said, "Tell me about your relationship with Melanie Chadwick."

Visibly shaken by the question, Humphrey tried to cover up with a casual nod and shrug. "We're old friends."

"Just friends?"

"Now. We were more than that a while back. Why do you ask?"

"I like to know who I'm working for, and why." Tony glared at him for a moment to let him know he wasn't happy. "You had Melanie check me out first, after you got my name from my friend, Joe Pellagreno. Since she's a broker, she can check into my background. Finances, employment, etc. What you might not have known, is that I could also find out who's been asking about me."

Humphrey look embarrassed. "Of course I'd have you checked out."

"And?"

"And you wouldn't be working for me if you weren't a good guy. I leave nothing to chance, Mr. Caruso."

Tony had a feeling that was the most truthful statement Cliff Humphrey would ever give him.

"You tell Melanie to fuck me also?"

"Hell no!" Humphrey's breathing became labored.

Tony closed his eyes, feeling like a complete idiot. Then he said, "What does it matter if your son killed his wife?"

Humphrey jumped to his feet and slammed his hand on the desk. "He didn't do it!"

Tony thought the man's arteries in his neck would explode. "Take it easy, Mr. Humphrey."

In a few seconds Humphrey slowly settled back into his chair and tried to calm his breathing. "I'm sorry," he said.

"I was just wondering how the truth would change things. It won't bring back your son."

He tightened his jaw. "I know that. But it will bring back his good name. I could never rest until I did that for Dan."

Maybe now wasn't a good time to bring up the fact that Cliff Humphrey stood to make out quite nicely, to the tune of a million bucks, if Tony found out his son was actually murdered. He could have brought that up, but he had already pissed the man off. Instead, he went in another direction.

"My reason for stopping by so early, is because I'd like to talk with the company vying for your son's company. Would you authorize that expense?"

"Of course, of course," Humphrey said. "Don't even ask questions like that. Just do it. I'll pay any and all expenses you submit after the fact. I just want the truth."

Tony had a feeling he'd say that, but he'd been burned in the past. Next, he changed his mind. Since Humphrey was already pissed off at him, he figured it couldn't get much worse. "Where were you the night Dan and Barb...were killed?" Tony asked him.

The question should have been quite disturbing. Enough for Humphrey to have a coronary. And enough for the sheriff to charge Tony with facilitating his death. But Humphrey didn't seem upset with the question.

"I expect questions like that from the sheriff," he said, "but not from someone who works for me." He hesitated. "However, since I've learned you pull no punches, I expected you to ask me that question the night I hired you. I was home. . .alone."

"Bugging me more than anything," Tony said, "is why your son would shoot his wife, then himself, and then set the gas fireplace to blow. That's overkill. And what would be the point?"

"Exactly!"

"I mean. . .they're dead. Why blow up the house?"

"Right. You believe me, then?"

It was hard not to believe him. Tony's Uncle Bruno had smelled it out in an instant. Maybe Tony wasn't cut out for this work. Well, he could just buy a small house on the Oregon coast and shoot photos—place them for sale in those little galleries in Lincoln City, Depoe Bay, and Cannon Beach. Sounded good about now.

"Let me keep digging," Tony said, and then left Humphrey in his office. As he was leaving, the receptionist and a few others were just arriving.

Next, Tony drove across the river to Deschutes Enterprises. He hesitated in the reception area waiting for Susie to get off the phone.

"Hi," she said, hanging the phone up. "Strange seeing you last night at Jamal's place."

"I have to talk with the neighbors when something tragic like that happens," Tony said, playing insurance investigator again. "Standard practice."

She smiled at him.

Tony continued, "You must be pretty good friends with Jamal to watch after his place for him like that."

"We met just a few days after he bought the place," she said. "I gave him the kitten. He adores it."

"How'd he hurt his ankle?"

"First time was a few weeks ago on a spinning jam. Came down wrong. He lost a week and a half. Then a few days ago some big guy landed on him during a rebound. Now he'll be out for another week or so."

"So, do you stay there all the time?"

She looked confused and disturbed at the same time. "I have my own place," she said with an edge. "I go over to feed the kitten and water the plants when Jamal's on the road. Are you here to see Mr. Gibson, or just to give me a hard time?" Her smile was somewhat strained.

"I'm sorry. I didn't mean to pry into your private life." He was as sincere as he could get.

She shrugged and formed a smile again. "That's okay."

Tony changed the subject. "Have you been to see Jamal play? I hear he's good."

"Yes, he is. I've been to a few games, but it's hard to get away. Who'd feed the cat?"

"Good point."

"I can get tickets any time," she said. "Maybe you'd like to go."

Tony assured her that he would. He had gotten the information he wanted, yet he didn't want her to know he had come there just to see her. So he asked to see Larry Gibson. Unfortunately he wasn't available. Tony looked disappointed as he left.

When he got back to his truck, Panzer was jumping around in the bed. He let out a couple of quick barks, which was rare for him.

"What's wrong with you? Need to take a piss?"

Tony went to the back end and opened the topper. Immediately, Panzer jumped from the back end and ran around the parking lot. He stopped on a strip of grass between parking sections and lifted his leg on a tree. Then the schnauzer ran toward the front of the parking lot, jumped into the grass in the first row of cars, and posed with his head pointed forward. Moments later, he started back toward Tony, but stopped at an Audi TT, sniffed for a second, and then took a piss on the left door.

"Panzer," Tony yelled quietly.

His dog's ears rose quickly and then the dog made a hasty return, jumping into the back end.

"Damn, boy. What the hell you thinking?"

Tony shook his head and climbed into his truck. He thought about what Susie had just told him. He got onto the cell phone, called information, and then punched in the Portland Trail Blazer front office. After making up some bogus story about being a freelance journalist working a story on the fragile ankle, some PR type finally came on and gave him the information he needed. Most important of all was the date that Jamal Banks was injured the first time. Two days before Dan and Barb Humphrey died. The PR person wouldn't give him Jamal's telephone number or address, referring him instead to the basketball player's agent in California. Tony got a hold of his agent, told him a similar story, and, although he was a busy man and extremely skeptical, he told Tony what he needed to know. Jamal had gone to Central Oregon after his injury to recuperate. That's all he'd said. Not Bend. No address. No telephone number. But what he didn't know, was that Tony already had all that information.

Why in the hell did it matter when the basketball player hurt himself? That's what Tony need to find out.

So Tony went out to Cascade Peaks Estates again. Parked in Jamal Banks' driveway, he sat for a minute, trying to figure out his line of questioning. Satisfied, he got out and went to the basketball player's front door.

This time he knocked and rang the door bell. Nothing.

When Tony heard a vehicle pull up, he turned and then shook his head realizing who it was. His two friends the MENSA brothers, playing dress-up as security guards. Tony walked back toward his truck to meet them, not in any mood to enter round three.

They got out, their hands on the ends of their nightsticks. Looking closely, they both still had remnants of their last two encounters. Flattop's nose was still larger and more crooked than normal, and Goatee's jaw was puffed out on one side.

Goatee was the first to speak. "Haven't you bothered these people enough, Caruso?"

"Not really. You see, when I wake up each morning I look at the calendar and a list of people. I make a note of those I haven't fucked with in a while and go directly to see them."

Neither of them said a word. No sense of humor. They would probably both die from stress-related heart attacks in their forties. If they didn't piss off somebody more dangerous and vindictive than Tony first.

Tony heard the front door to the house open. He backed up a few steps and turned to see the basketball player, Jamal Banks, standing there in his trunks, holding his kitten.

"What da fuck's goin' on out there?" he yelled at the three of them. When he saw Tony he smiled and waved his hand at him. "Hey, Tony. How the hell's it hangin'?"

"These two Bozos don't want me talking to you," Tony said, turning to glare at the two of them.

"Hey," Jamal screeched. "You rent-a-fucks get da hell outta here and let me talk to my Tony." He was waving his hand at the two of them like he would to swat away a couple of pesky gnats.

Tony laughed as he watched the two of them, tails tucked between their legs, climb into their truck and back out. He went in to talk with Jamal.

CHAPTER 23

"Ya want some coffee?" Jamal asked. He was stretched out on the leather sofa in the living room like a drunken cowboy who had mistakenly straddled a heifer.

Tony hesitated and then took a seat across a marble-topped table with a few copies of Architectural Digest magazine prominently displayed. "No, thanks, Jamal. I just stopped by because I forgot to ask you a few things last night."

"Just a sec," he said. He stretched across the sofa to a game controller and a remote. Then he clicked on the T.V. and switched over to a Playstation 2 car racing game. "Okay. Now I'm set."

Tony shifted in his chair, catching the racing action from the corner of his eye. "Your ankle... I understand you hurt it doing some spectacular jam?"

"Motherfucker!"

"What?"

"Not you, man." He stretched out his skinny finger at the T.V. "I fuckin' crashed."

"Your ankle?"

He hesitated. "That's part of the game." He put special emphasis on that last word, and then said, "The fans don't wanna see a bunch of pussies clomping up the hardwood with that lay-up shit. They want some air."

Tony couldn't have agreed more with him. He always thought if the women really wanted fan support, they would lower the baskets to nine feet and start jamming the crap out of the ball. "What I meant was, you were injured two days before Dan and Barb Humphrey died." Tony turned slightly, watching Jamal's car fly around the track and sift through the cars. Since he didn't respond, Tony continued. "You were here, Jamal. The night they died. The night their house blew up."

Jamal's car smashed into the grandstands. "Shiiit..."

"Jamal?"

He shook his head and set the game controller down. "What the fuck you want from me?"

"I just want to know if you saw anything out of the ordinary that night."

"Yeah. Damn straight. It ain't normal for a frickin' house to blow up."

Tony had that one coming. Almost the same thing Mrs. Ellison had said when he asked her that question. "Did you hear a shot prior to the place going up?"

He thought for a moment. "What? You think 'cause I'm black I be used to hearing gunshots?"

"Cut the bullshit, Jamal. You grew up in a nice north Chicago suburb, one of two children of a prominent cardiac surgeon mother and a father who was a lawyer at one of the largest firms in that city. After high school, you went to Stanford on a full scholarship. Scored almost 1500 on your SATs. The attitude is an act, my friend."

Jamal sat with his jaw shifted to one side.

Tony continued, "I'm sorry. I just thought maybe you heard something and looked out your window."

Jamal laughed out loud, pointing his finger at Tony. "I had ya going, Tony, my man." He restarted his game, and when the lights went from red to green, he jammed his thumb onto the button as if he was really behind the wheel of the race car.

"Did you see anything that night?"

"I don't pay attention to other people's business."

Time to lead the witness. "What about a car?"

He let out a gasp of air. "Aw right. I saw a car."

"What kind?"

"It was dark." His race car smashed into another car and flipped over. Luckily, the program popped it back over for him. "If I had to guess, I'd say it was a Ford. Some piece of shit like that."

"Anything else?"

He paused the game and stared right at Tony. "Yeah, the fuckin' second shooter on the grassy knoll." Shaking his head, he continued the game.

Tony had a feeling there was something else he wasn't telling him, but he also knew he was starting to piss him off. And if he wanted anything else, he needed to lay off. Tony thanked him for the information and saw himself out.

When he got to the truck, Captain Beaver Jackson was parked in his truck just behind Tony's vehicle. He got out and shuffled up to him, his expression sullen, like he was about to do something totally against his nature. Stopping a few feet from Tony, the captain pulled his pants up higher on his waist.

Tony had a feeling he knew what was coming. The good captain had been forced to sit through the crying of his two men and now felt somewhat compelled to act.

"What can I do for you, Mr. Jackson?" Tony said.

The security captain twisted his neck to the side, cracking it as easily as some would their knuckles. "I hope I don't have to go to the sheriff to keep you from hassling our residents." He gave Tony a slight smile to show he wasn't absolutely pissed off at him. At least not yet.

"Don't think that'll be a problem," Tony said. He thought about it for a second, and then said, "Has somebody complained about me?"

"Can't say."

"You've obviously been talking with those two Einsteins of yours."

He laughed and then pulled out a piece of gum from his pocket, offered Tony one, and when he waved him off, Beaver Jackson shrugged and shoved a piece into his mouth. "Doctor told me to stop smoking," he said. "It's a damn conspiracy. They're all in it together." He hesitated as Tony gave him a blank stare. "The doctors and dentists. Doctor says don't smoke, chew gum. Got two choices there. Sugar gum, which rots your teeth, and sugar free, which causes cancer. Doctors'll get you back one way or another. They got ya coming into this world, ya gotta pay 'em all along the way, and then ya pay 'em when you're dying." He shook his head like he'd just said the most profound thing in his life. With the gum back in his molars, he was chomping away like a cow.

Wasn't much Tony could say. "I think I've talked with everyone I need to at Cascade Peaks," he said.

"That so?"

"At least for now. I needed to talk with Jamal Banks...since he was here the night Dan and Barb died."

Beaver Jackson lowered his brows as if Tony was a quarterback and he was about to run right over his center and take off his head. "Thought he was playing in Portland that night," he said, without much conviction.

"No. He'd already injured his ankle. Just told me that himself."

"What else he have to say?"

"I'm afraid that's confidential," Tony said. "Let's just say I'm getting closer to the truth."

Tony got into the truck and lowered the window.

Beaver Jackson stood back a few feet, his hands on his hips.

"You need to keep an eye on those two gifted children of yours," Tony said. "They might try to bite off more than they can chew. Good way to choke." Tony smiled and turned his head toward the captain's truck, which sat in Tony's way.

Jackson took that as a sign to move out of Tony's way. He shuffled off and moved his vehicle.

Backing out, Tony smiled and waved at the good captain as he left.

Tony had just made it through the front gate when he got a call on his cell phone from Sheriff Bill Green. He wanted to see him right away. Now! Great.

CHAPTER 24

Tony would have expected the sheriff to haul him into his office, plant him into an uncomfortable chair, and proceed to chew his ass for something or other. But that didn't happen. In fact, he had asked him nicely to meet him in Drake Park in downtown Bend, right on the same bridge where Tony and Dawn Sanders had stood the other day.

Parking on the west bank of the Deschutes River, Tony walked a block to the meeting. Panzer took this opportunity, once again, to chase after geese at a safe distance, and generally frolic about the wide green spaces. The sheriff was already waiting for him, leaning against a rail and not even turning to look at him as Tony approached.

"What's up?" Tony said.

His eyes shifted toward Tony. "A couple of my deputies were called out to the Riverfront condos this morning. There was a condo last used by a Frank Peroni completely destroyed. Someone at the front desk told us about how a man claiming to be his brother had been there. You wouldn't know anything about that?"

Leaning against the bridge rail next to the sheriff, Tony shrugged. "They didn't talk to you?"

The sheriff turned quickly. "Who?"

"The two Portland Police detectives. Shabato and Reese. I caught them rifling through Peroni's condo."

"The guy at the front desk didn't say anything about two cops," he said. "He described you like a photo, though."

"And after I said I'd pay the bill."

"What?"

"I told Shabato and Reese you might want to get together, considering all the break-ins around here you told me about."

The sheriff had an incredulous glare across his face. "Again, Tony. Why are the Portland detectives running around Deschutes County?"

"I have no idea. I went to Portland to hunt down Frank Peroni. Back up. I found out Frank Peroni went home with Dan and Barb Humphrey the night the house was blown to shit. I went to Portland to find Peroni. He wasn't there. His wife said he hasn't been back from Bend. Filed a missing person report; the whole nine yards. I leave Peroni's place and pick up a tail. It's the Portland cops, Shabato and Reese. They say they like Peroni for a string of robberies in upscale neighborhoods there. Entering but no breaking. They figure Peroni sold the locks and security systems and then hired someone to go in later. Sweet deal."

"No shit. Ream their ass coming and going. Sounds like something a lawyer would do."

"Yeah, I also thought about your problem here. You mentioned the problems you've had." Tony shrugged.

Letting out a deep breath, the sheriff said, "I'll call Portland. But I have another concern." He slid his large frame sideways toward Tony. "This thing you're looking into. Dan and Barb Humphrey. The autopsy came back from Portland, and as I suspected, everything was as I guessed it would be. Dental matches. Their wedding rings. Everything."

"What about DNA?"

His eyes narrowed on Tony. "There was no reason for that. No reason for us to believe they weren't who we thought they were."

Tony started to back away. "Gotcha."

"One more thing," the sheriff said.

Tony stopped and looked at the sheriff.

"Leave the residents alone out at Cascade Peaks."

Letting out a slight laugh, Tony said, "I have everything I need from that place. I thought you might have actually found out something about the person who shot me. How's that investigation going?"

He smiled and shrugged. "You didn't give us much to go on."

Tony gave a little whistle and Panzer came running and stopped at his feet.

"I heard you had a giant schnauzer."

"Yeah, and I've got a big dog, too."

"I heard they're used in Germany for police work," the sheriff said. "This one trained?"

Tony stooped down and rubbed Panzer behind the ears. "He doesn't piss in the house, if that's what ya mean."

The sheriff shook his head as he started to walk away. "You take care of yourself, Tony," he said over his shoulder.

Watching the sheriff drift back along the fake cobblestones toward downtown, Tony got down on one knee next to his dog. He didn't need the sheriff telling him that. Enough had happened in the past few days to keep his senses at peak performance. But something had bothered him about this whole case. Something he had contemplated on his drive to see the sheriff.

"You'll take care of me," he said to Panzer.

The dog whined and yawned.

"Always vigilant. How'd you like to see our favorite acupuncturist?"

He went back to his truck, loaded Panzer into the back, and then headed toward her place.

When he got to the Naturopathic Clinic, the receptionist informed him that Dawn Sanders wasn't there. She had gone out to her brother's house in a hurry, not saying why. That was almost a half an hour ago, she said.

Tony got directions to Don Sanders' place out on Mount Jefferson Drive. Driving out there, he passed tall stands of old growth ponderosa pines mingled with swatches of sage and virgin juniper. The road rose up as he neared the location, and he could see immediately why Cliff Humphrey and his partners wanted to build a resort there. Spreading out to the west and north were unobstructed panoramic views of Mount Bachelor, Broken Top, the Three Sisters, and he suspected from farther out in the fields to the west, some sites would have views of Mount Jefferson and Mount Washington.

Tony pulled into the dirt driveway and parked behind a Toyota 4x4 pickup. Up closer to the house was a larger white Chevy truck, with the back enclosed with a specially designed container with locked doors and explosives symbols plastered to the side. Don Sanders' work truck that Tony had seen out at the blast site.

He got out and looked around. Panzer was going nuts in the back of the truck.

"Settle down, Panzer. I know what you smell."

The dog circled around a few times, his nose in the air, and finally settled into his bed.

The house wasn't anything special. A little ranch house fifty or sixty years old, with a cedar shake roof and siding that needed a coat of stain. Surrounding the house were shrubs that had gotten carried away, spreading branches in front of the windows. He went to the front door and knocked. Nothing. He tried looking through the window, but couldn't see anyone inside. Then he noticed it. The frame alongside the lock had been pried and ripped away. Probably how someone had gotten into the place. Looking more closely, Tony noticed the lock. It was a Cascade Lock.

Suddenly, Tony heard a muffled voice around the corner of the house. He stepped down from the stoop and made his way around the side of the building. Then the voice became more clear. A man. Don Sanders? The voice was coming from a small out-building that might have been a barn of some sort. He guessed as much, since there was a dilapidated fence that led out from each side of the wooden frame, and then out farther to a trampled and well eaten pasture.

"Motherfucker!" the voice said as Tony got closer.

Then there was a second voice. A woman. Consoling. Dawn Sanders. Tony got to a gate, slipped through it, and closed it behind him.

"Bastards. Motherfuckin' bastards. I'll kill that fucker."

Tony slowed a bit when he heard that.

"You can't prove he did this," Dawn said.

Tony made his way around the side of the building and understood immediately why Don Sanders was so angry. Laying on the ground on its side was a horse, its belly bloated like somebody had shoved a helium hose up its ass and started filling it up. Tony stopped and looked down, almost stepping in a huge pile of manure.

Dawn and Don both turned to look at him. She was wearing a pair of blue jeans and hiking boots, a western shirt tucked into her pants. It was a look that totally surprised Tony, considering how she had appeared up to this point. Her brother wore coveralls and steal-toed boots. He yanked on his long beard when he saw Tony.

"What the fuck you doin' here?" he yelled out at Tony.

"Don!" she said. She stepped closer and gazed up at Tony without the use of her little round spectacles. She was wearing tinted contacts that made her green eyes seem like smooth chunks of jade. "How'd you find me?" she asked.

"I stopped by your office. Thought you might want to do lunch." Tony glanced around her. "What happened to the horse?"

Her brother stomped closer. "I'll tell you what happened. Some cowardly motherfucker shot my mare. I come home for a little lunchtime chow and find this." He waved his hand at the distended gray mare.

"Who?" Tony asked.

"Who the fuck you think?" Don Sanders ran his fingers though his hair. When Tony didn't answer, he said, "Humphrey!" He spit his client's name out like it was bile that had bubbled up from his gut.

"You don't know that, Donny," she said, placing her hand on

her brother's arm.

"Who else?" Don Sanders said. It was obvious she had a calming effect on him.

She didn't say a thing. Didn't have an answer for him.

"We been through so much together," he said, gazing at the mare like a husband would to a wife who had died. "We were out there." He swished his hand out to no place in particular toward the mountains. "When they came." He smiled at Tony.

His sister shook her head. "Donny let's not go there again."

Tony was confused. "Who came?"

"Don't ask," she said.

"I'll tell you who," Don Sanders said. "Our friends. They don't wanna do us no harm. They're just curious."

Tony was about to open his mouth when he saw Dawn shake her head at him.

"Them," Don whispered. "I was riding the mare out there one night. Three years ago. I saw the light. I felt this feeling of rising up into the sky." He sighed as if he missed the experience, wanted it to happen to him all over again.

Tony let him talk because it was taking his mind off the mare.

Without warning, Don Sanders drifted over to his mare, knelt down, and wrapped his arms around the horse's neck.

His sister pulled Tony aside. "We think he fell off his horse that night," she explained. "I found him out in the field the next morning when he didn't show up to work, the mare standing next to him, and he was hypothermic. The doctor said he had a fractured skull. He hasn't been the same since."

"Don't you go planting lies into his head," her brother said, getting to his feet and drifting toward the two of them. "I haven't lost it yet. Humphrey ripped me off to try to drive me off this place. Wiped me out. Even took supplies so I couldn't work."

That got Tony's attention. "Like what?"

He shrugged. "Actuators. Wire. Some chemicals. Not everything. Just enough to slow me down. I had to drive to Portland to buy more."

Now that was interesting. Could have explained the matching wire at Don's work site and the Humphrey house.

"I think you should have a vet look at the mare," Tony said. "Pull the slug out. See what kind of gun shot her."

Don nodded his head at Tony.

Tony and Dawn walked back to the front of the house. She seemed concerned.

"What do you think?" Tony asked her.

She stopped a few feet from her Toyota 4x4 and turned to Tony. Her eyes were uncertain. "I don't know. I'd like to think that Cliff Humphrey wouldn't do something like this. My God. This is Oregon. It's almost as bad to kill a horse as a human." She let out a heavy sigh.

"But?"

"But...I guess it's possible. I mean, who else would have killed his horse?" Then she pointed off toward her brother's house. "My grandparents built this place sixty years ago. We were brought up out here, back when Bend was a quiet little town. Now the place has grown beyond recognition. And my brother." She thought for a moment, shaking her head from side to side. "He doesn't fully understand the development, yet he's become a part of it. I think that bothers him on some level."

She seemed on the verge of crying. Tony stepped closer, unsure if he should take her in his arms.

"What about the break-in here?" Tony asked. "I noticed the door frame was ripped apart."

"Did you look inside?"

"No."

"There's nothing in there. Whoever came here took everything. Even his damn phone. Donny hasn't even had a chance to replace anything. He's sleeping on the floor. He blames himself. He would have been home, but he was given a pair of tickets for a Blazers game. This is an isolated place. Someone must have brought a truck up and just piled his stuff in. The silly thing is, he didn't have a lot of good things. I mean, nothing of great value. I just know someone did it to force a deal with Humphrey."

"Who knew he was going to the Blazers game?" Tony asked.

"Probably not many people. He doesn't do much socializing anymore. Not since his accident."

"The fall from the horse?" Tony said.

"Yeah."

Tony had more to ask her, but not here. They decided to do lunch, driving separate to a nice Mexican place downtown.

CHAPTER 25

Having finished their lunch, Tony and Dawn sat for a moment staring at each other. She had a glass of red wine, and Tony had a local microbrew. Their conversation over lunch had dealt with what he was currently working on, and her brother. Somehow he had a feeling Don Sanders was involved, however remotely, with the whole Dan and Barb Humphrey and Frank Peroni situation. Their conversation just turned to Peroni.

"I don't see what that guy has to do with anything," she said, taking a sip of wine, but keeping her eyes on Tony.

"I'm not entirely convinced myself. As far as Dan and Barb are concerned, I think Peroni saw something. Something that made him go into hiding."

Tony sat there thinking about Frank Peroni and what Detective Shabato and Reese had told him about the man. How Peroni was under investigation for robberies in the Portland area. How his boss had reacted when Tony talked with him. Considering everything he knew, Tony had an idea. He needed to get back to his condo and his computer to check out his theory.

Tony's cell phone rang. He reluctantly picked it up. "Yeah."

"What the hell, Tony. Someone shoots you and I gotta find out a couple of days later?"

"Uncle Bruno." Tony lowered his voice and said, "It's not like I'd put out a press release. It was a grazing shot. A few stitches." Tony shrugged to Dawn across the table.

"You get your ass to Duluth for Christmas. I won't take no for an answer. All your cousins will be there. Sounds like you could use a break."

Tony shook his head. "I gotta finish this first. I think I'm gettin' close."

"Somebody thinks so."

"Bruno, I gotta get going. I'm at lunch with a beautiful woman."

"Well. . .carry on then."

Smiling, Tony clicked off the phone and put it into his pocket.

"Sorry about that. My Uncle Bruno wants me to go to Minnesota for Christmas."

"No problem. I'm a beautiful woman?" She smiled.

Rising from his chair, Tony threw enough money on the table to cover lunch. But their departure from the restaurant would be delayed. Walking across the room directly toward them, at a pace that made her determined expression somewhat sinister, was Melanie Chadwick. She was wearing a short gray skirt that slid up her firm legs with each step. She stopped at their table and crossed her arms over her white silk blouse. Tony took his seat again.

"I was wondering if you planned on calling me," Melanie said, her eyes narrowing toward Tony. "Now I see why you won't." Her glare shifted toward Dawn, who looked embarrassed, which Tony didn't think was part of her facial repertoire.

"There's nothing going on between us, Melanie," Dawn said.

"Right." Melanie's foot started tapping, like a mother would do listening to a child try to lie his way out of a fix.

"Why don't you sit down," Tony said. "We were just discussing what I was working on."

"I think I know what you're working on, Tony." She raised her brows, but she wasn't smiling.

Tony was aware of people staring at them. Not that he cared much about that. But he was somewhat embarrassed for the two of them, since they had to do business in Bend.

Tony got up and Dawn rose after him. Then Tony saw a woman sitting against the far wall, her eyes gazing directly at the commotion of Dawn, Melanie and himself. Mrs. James Ellison. She smiled at him just like she had the last time he had seen her, rising up naked from the hot tub, imploring him to enter and join her.

Without saying another word, the three of them went out to the front of the building. Tony expected a long recitation on how he was a pig like every other man on the planet. And maybe he had it coming, because he wasn't able to convince himself that he didn't have feelings for Dawn Sanders. What he got was far less biting.

Melanie calmly looked Tony in the eye and said, "I should have known better than to get involved with another Italian. Always thinking with the little head." Then she simply turned and walked away.

Ouch. A personal attack was one thing. But to attack his heritage...that hurt, Tony thought

Dawn stepped closer to Tony and took his hand in hers. "Believe me. From what I've seen, the little head is not that little."

They both started laughing.

Tony had agreed to keep in touch with Dawn. He wanted to see more of her, and that wasn't the little head thinking. She was a beautiful, interesting person. Someone who he thought would be a friend over time.

On the way back to the condo, he took a quick detour toward the river, parking next to Cliff Humphrey's Mercedes out front of his development company. As he walked into the building, he tried to prepare himself for the questions he had to ask him. Questions that would surely strain their relationship, whatever that was.

Inside, he breezed right past the receptionist, past a man and a woman discussing something at a drafting table, and stormed into

Cliff Humphrey's office, slamming the door behind him.

Humphrey was surprised and shocked to see him. He started to get up from behind his desk, when Tony pointed his finger right at him, sending him back into the leather.

"I'm sick of being lied to," Tony yelled. He hesitated, trying to build tension.

When Cliff Humphrey didn't say anything, Tony continued. "You know Frank Peroni."

He had a stupid look on his face, and Tony knew he was searching his mind for the lie of the minute.

"Well?"

Letting out a deep sigh, Humphrey said, "I don't understand how that matters."

Tony leaned onto the man's desk and tightened his jaw. "You let me decide what's pertinent to the case. I asked you the other day if you knew him, and you lied to me. Why?"

Humphrey slid his hands together as if he were praying. Good. Maybe Tony was actually scaring the guy into asking for God's help.

"I'm sure Mr. Peroni had nothing to do with Dan and Barb's death," Humphrey said, each word spoken deliberately.

"What makes you so sure?"

"What motive would he have?"

Technicality. Unfortunately, he had a point, and Tony let him know that by loosening his grip on his desk. But he also knew that motives came in flimsy forms quite often. Tony had a feeling there were too many people with too much money involved with this case. He was convinced of that much.

"Why didn't you tell me Frank Peroni had sold locks to damn near every development you built?" Tony asked.

"It wasn't relevant." Humphrey's voice had an edge to it now, as if the power was shifting back to him.

"He was at the house the night your son died," Tony said. "That's relevant."

"Says who?"

"Says me." Tony backed away from the desk, turned, and started to leave.

"Have you even talked with the man?" Humphrey asked.

Tony stopped and turned. "No. But I plan on it. You hired me to find out what happened. If you can't handle the truth, you should have hired some hack." With that, Tony stormed out of the office just as he had entered.

On the way out to the truck, everything was jumbling in his mind. He wasn't sure what he was investigating any more. He was working for some lying bastard he was beginning to hate. Which shouldn't have been a problem, except he promised himself when he got into this whole business that he wouldn't take a job from some high maintenance puke like Humphrey and he had broken his own rule. Tony could only comfort himself by knowing that his real clients were dead. Dan and Barb. He was completely convinced now that they both had been murdered. His task now was to prove who killed them.

Frank Peroni was key to the whole deal. He knew that much. He drove back to the condo, thinking he had a pretty good idea how to find the man.

Tony had been at the condo for about an hour when the snow started falling. It was late afternoon, heading into early evening. He had been locked onto the computer, searching the net for some clue on how to find Peroni. Having pulled out a map of the county and circling the locations where Frank Peroni had taken out cash advances against his Visa, he had a reasonable idea where he was. Frank had made a few errors. He had thought it was safe to go to resorts to draw the cash. Rightfully so. But by doing so, he had given up his relative location. He wouldn't want to drive very far, thinking the cops might be looking for his car.

So, how to narrow down his hiding place? Make a bunch of phone calls and computer checks.

A few hours later, through periods of frustration and uncertainty, Tony thought he might have actually gotten a solid lead. He had talked with Frank's wife, talked with resort personnel, talked with grocery store clerks, talked with damn near anyone who would talk. In the end, he found a telephone number that might have been helpful. The address where the phone was located was probably even more significant, since it was owned by one James Burton, the marketing director he had talked with at Cascade Lock in Beaverton. Frank's boss.

Tony gathered up a few things before heading out. Put on his hiking boots, winter coat and gloves, and his ski hat.

By the time he got to the truck, darkness had settled across Central Oregon, and six inches of fresh powder had fallen already. He switched on the radio after clearing the windows of snow, and an overly enthusiastic woman informed him the entire area was under a winter storm advisory. Great. On the bright side, the radio lady had said, skiing in the morning would be excellent. The silver lining.

He considered leaving Panzer in the condo, but he had no idea how long this would take. Besides, the dog had shown a great fondness to snow.

Placing the dog behind the seat in the cab with him, Tony dropped the truck into four-wheel-drive and pulled out into the blowing sheet of white. He had no idea if his hunch would turn up anything more than a winter driving lesson. But he had to try. He was running out of options.

CHAPTER 26

The road toward Black Butte was treacherous. Tony's only consolation was that not many people were out and about. Only other crazy bastards like him, he thought, with four wheel drive and the brains of the village idiot.

He passed Black Butte Ranch, an expansive resort and golf community, and one of the places Frank Peroni had gotten cash. Farther on down the road, he slowed the truck to watch for signs. Having memorized the map before leaving, he knew he needed to take a right toward Camp Sherman.

He almost missed the sign, sliding around the corner and fish-tailing a few times before straightening it out. He didn't have much information about James Burton's second home. He imagined it was a summer cabin, but he wasn't about to call the guy and ask him. He wanted to see the look on Frank Peroni's face when he saw him, before someone had a chance to say he had called. Who knows? Frank would have probably bolted.

Fifteen minutes later he passed through Camp Sherman, which wasn't really a town, but a quick stop for people who owned second homes in the area. There was a gas station, a volunteer firehouse, and a small general store. He had contacted the store hoping to find information about Frank Peroni. Bingo. The clerk had told him about a man fitting Peroni's description. They were used to strangers in the area. Hunters. Fishermen. But most of them came through in the summer or fall, not December. And this guy had been there a few times in the past two weeks. Always nervous, she had said.

Tony continued on along the road until it crossed the Metolius River. Melanie Chadwick had told him that there were million dollar homes along the river. She had listed a number of the places. Decadent opulence is how she had described some of the places there. But he saw none of that in the snowstorm. He was having a rough enough time keeping the truck on the road.

After he crossed the river, the road narrowed even more, and he knew that Burton's place was supposed to be the second road on the left and would probably angle back toward the river.

There it was. He slowed and turned onto a dirt lane that was covered now with almost a foot of new snow, his headlights glistening off the pine boughs weighted to the breaking point.

He had no idea how far the private drive went from the main road to the house. Nor did he even know for sure if he'd find Frank Peroni there. He did know that if he was there, and Tony parked the truck in the middle of the driveway, there was no way he would be able to get his Ford Taurus past him. In fact, Peroni would have been lucky to move the car a few feet in that thick, wet snow.

Which gave him an idea. Figuring he was getting closer, he turned the F250 at an angle across the lane where it narrowed between two trees. Then he shut down the engine and got out.

Panzer tried to jump out with him. *"Nein! Sitzen."*

Closing the door on Panzer, Tony flicked on a small penlight briefly to make sure it worked, and then shoved into his jacket pocket. He zipped up his jacket, pulled his hat over his ears, and trudged off through the snow.

Tony always found something serene about walking through fresh snow in the darkness, the fluffy flakes settling lightly on his head and shoulders. One flake would catch an eyelash and he would blink it away. As a kid growing up in northern Minnesota, Tony would get bundled up during a good evening snowstorm, lay on his back, and let the snow cover him. Strange how the mind worked, he thought. He should have been thinking about Frank Peroni and how he related to Dan and Barb Humphrey getting killed, but he was feeling the snow against his face as he trudged forward.

The road curved a few times and he could hear the Metolius River rippling in the distance, the sloshing of water clearer and clearer as he made his way down the road.

Then Tony saw it. A faint light in the distance, the snow falling in blankets in front of it. He stepped softly toward the light. Seconds later he could see a car. The Ford Taurus? Maybe his guess had been right. He came up to the rear of the car and swiped his hand across the trunk, knocking a thick patch of snow away. Yep. Ford Taurus. Then he thought about what Peroni's wife had told him, so he went to the front of the car and brushed away some of the snow from the windshield. There was a long crack.

When he turned toward the house, a figure appeared in the window. Just as quickly, the man was gone.

The house was built of logs, resembling a mountain cabin that could have been made to look like a settler's home, but was actually quite new, Tony could tell. The construction was too perfect. The logs too precisely cut, they looked like Lincoln Logs.

As Tony made his way toward the front porch, he wondered if he was doing the right thing. What if Peroni had killed Dan and Barb and was hiding out before skipping the country? He could have been dangerous, not thinking twice about killing Tony as well. He felt the flashlight in his pocket and thought about carrying a gun next time. But first he'd have to buy one.

He stepped lightly up the wooden stairs, trying not to make any noise. When he reached the door, which was wooden half way up and then glass panes the rest of the way, he could see more lights inside. A T.V. shone in the large open space, and a fire flashed its flames in a huge stone fireplace. Sitting in a leather chair, flipping through channels much like his wife had done in Portland, was a man in sweats and a sweater; one foot housed in a Nike basketball shoe hung over the chair's arm dangling back and forth. The man took a swig of beer from a long neck bottle before flipping the channel again.

Tony checked the door knob. It was locked. Then he noticed that there was an electronic lock as well as a mechanical dead bolt. Both said Cascade Lock on them. Figured.

Looking back along the driveway at Peroni's car, Tony realized there wasn't anyplace the guy could go. Just knock and talk. So he did just that.

He thought that Frank Peroni would piss his pants when he heard the first knock. He nearly jumped out of the chair. Then, gathering courage, he rose to his feet and strut across the wooden floor. He stopped and flicked the light on Tony to get a closer look.

Then he said, "Who the fuck are you?"

And he thought Peroni's wife had given him the cold shoulder. "I'm Tony Caruso."

The man's brows rose unexpectedly. "What do you want with me?" he yelled through the glass.

"Are you Frank Peroni?" he asked, even though he recognized him from the picture at his house in Portland.

"What's it to you?"

This was going great. "Could I come in and talk with you for a minute? It's kind of nasty out here." Tony shivered for effect.

He looked Tony over, probably figured he was harmless, much like the two rent-a-cops had, and then opened the door for him. Tony stomped and wiped the snow from his boots and pants and then followed Peroni into the living room. Stopping next to the fire, Tony turned toward Peroni, who was back in his chair. Peroni put on a music station and then set the remote on the end table.

"Let me guess," he said. "My wife hired you to find me?"

He couldn't have been serious. "What?"

He stared at Tony with a stupid expression, like he just stepped on a pile of dog crap and he was wondering how to get it off his shoe. "My wife didn't hire you?"

Tony assured him she had not. Then he said, "What have you been doing the last two weeks?"

"What are you, my mother?" He killed off the last of his beer and then got up and went to the refrigerator for another. He took a seat again and downed a third of the bottle.

Tony had to get right to the point. See how he reacted. "You went home with Dan and Barb Humphrey the night they were killed."

He narrowed his eyebrows at Tony. He was a worse actor than his boss, James Burton. "I don't know these people."

"I've got your finger prints at the scene, along with your DNA from pubic hair." Tony let that sink in for a few seconds. Hey, what the hell, he was a better actor than Peroni. A better liar, too.

He shook his head side to side. "No frickin' way. I don't know what you're talkin' about."

"You are one pathetic liar. I've got witnesses saying you left the Riverfront with Dan and Barb. The next day you drop off the face of the earth. Either you killed them or you know who did. Which is it?"

He ran his fingers through his hair and let out a heavy sigh. "Motherfucker. I just try to get a little pussy..." He trailed off, taking another swig of beer.

"What happened, Frank?"

Peroni thought about it for a second or two. Tony had a feeling the guy wasn't involved with their death, but he knew who was. He also knew that he probably hadn't talked with anyone about what had happened in the past two weeks, and that was driving him crazy. He was scared, Tony could tell.

"I was at the Riverfront that night," he started. "Minding my own business, I'll have you know. Then this beautiful woman comes up and sits next to me, offers to buy me a drink. I'm gonna refuse that? Hell no! In no time she's all over me like a politician on a girl scout. She's got her hand on my crotch. You name it."

Peroni thought for a moment, drank his beer, but kept his eyes on Tony. He continued. "So after a while she asks if I want to go back to her place to party. I don't refuse."

"What about her husband?" Tony asked.

"Hold onto your dick. I'm getting to that. Just before we get up to go, this guy shows up. I figure it's just someone she knows. But she comes right out and says it's her husband. I'm ready to bolt, until the guy asks if I'd like to fuck his wife. Let me tell you something, she was something to look at. It was kinda kinky, but under the circumstances, I wasn't about to refuse. He assured me he didn't want to suck my dick or anything like that. Just wanted to watch. Got off on that shit, I guess. I never had an audience before, but I'm an open kinda guy. So we left."

Tony was feeling the warmth from the fireplace and thinking about his last encounter with Melanie Chadwick. "Then you went back to their house at Cascade Peaks Estates?"

"Yeah. I wasn't sure if I could perform under those conditions." He smiled broadly, obviously remembering his moment of glory.

"So you and Barb do it while Dan watches? Then what?"

"She was beautiful. I never had a woman like her. Tremendous body. We did it a few times while her old man tries to beat the meat in the corner. Then she tells me to go outside to the hot tub. I figured she was gonna give her husband a shot at that pussy. So I go."

Suddenly, Tony saw a flash of light coming from outside. At least he thought that's what it was.

"What you looking at?" Peroni said, gazing off toward the front door.

"I thought I saw something out there. A light."

Frank Peroni got up quickly. "Someone followed you here."

The next couple of flashes weren't from flashlights. They were from guns going off. In their direction.

CHAPTER 27

They didn't have time for anything. Bullets had crashed through the glass on the front door, sending shards onto the wooden floor. Tony grabbed Frank Peroni by the arm and then the two of them raced through the kitchen, snatching his winter coat on the way out the back door.

As the door flung shut behind them, Tony could hear the front door smash in, and knew it would be only seconds before the shooters were right behind them.

They jumped from the wooden deck in the back into a growing snow bank. Tony was disoriented and unsure where to go, but moved through the deep snow with purpose downhill. Frank was right at his side.

The back door swung open and Tony waited for shots. Nothing. Then he heard a voice yelling, like one giving another orders.

They slipped and slid down the hill, branches from pines whipping them in the face. Frank fell and his body careened down the embankment for ten feet before he caught himself, digging his feet into the thick snow, and then raised himself to his feet again.

Tony thought of pulling his flashlight from his pocket, but realized they'd be perfect targets for the shooters.

Crashing down the hill behind them, Tony could hear at least two men.

Water roared ahead of them. They had to slow down or they'd go flying into the Metolius River.

The river was getting closer, the noise of frigid water sloshing over rocks just below them. Tony was afraid they'd come to a cliff, which was so common in the area, and crash over the edge to their death.

But his eyes had adjusted somewhat to the darkness, and he could see something shimmering ahead through the falling snow.

Suddenly the hill leveled down and they hit bottom, their legs collapsing beneath them. Frank yelled in pain. Tony rolled as if he had just hit the ground while parachuting.

Tony got to his feet and pulled the flashlight from his pocket, narrowing the beam toward Frank through cupped hands. He was holding his left ankle.

"You all right?" Tony whispered, out of breath.

"I think so." Peroni was panting as if he'd just run a mile. "Bad sprain."

Tony listened carefully. The men were still coming, perhaps slower than the two of them had descended the hill, though.

Tony pulled Frank to his feet. "Let's go."

He struggled against him. "Where? We're out in the middle of nowhere."

"You wanna stay here and get shot?"

Tony flashed the light down the edge of the river toward what looked like a deer trail, trampled down even more by fly fishermen. Shutting off the light, they ran off down stream.

Leading the way at a jogger's pace, Tony tried to keep his footing in the deep, heavy snow. It was like tromping through wet oatmeal.

After a short while, Tony could hear one man talking to the other. They had reached the bottom. Tony turned to see that they had a light and could simply follow their tracks. Damn!

As they ran, Tony asked Frank, "How deep is the river?"

"No fuckin' way," Frank said. "You're not gettin' me in there. We'd be dead in a minute."

"How deep is it?"

"I don't know."

They kept going. Maybe they could outrun them. Problem was, Tony wasn't even sure who they were or why they were after them. Nor did he have much time to speculate on the subject. He was acting on instincts now. And he knew that if they didn't do something, the shooters could catch them, or at least get close enough to start shooting again.

Without warning, Tony grabbed Frank and shoved him to the right. Then he followed Peroni into the river.

Crashing into the water, the icy waves enveloped Tony, taking his breath away. He recalled going under, hitting something hard on the bottom, and then rising to the surface. But he still had Frank by his collar, who then took in water and started choking.

They rode the rapids for a while, their bodies going numb, and then in a moment the noise from the river seemed to fade in the distance behind them as the river widened.

Tony shoved his leg down and felt rocks, so he planted his hiking boots and hoisted his body upward, bringing Frank Peroni with him. Frank had stopped coughing now, but he was shivering uncontrollably. So was Tony.

"What the hell'd you do that for?" Frank chattered through his teeth.

They waded toward shore. Tony's face and neck ached as the cold wind hit his exposed skin. He didn't know how far they had floated. But, just as they got to shore, there was a set of headlights that seemed to float across the river downstream. The bridge. The one he had crossed on the way to the cabin. That meant the road would be up the embankment. They had to get there and backtrack to his truck.

Tony tried to explain to Frank his plan as they ran up the steep hill toward the road, but he wasn't sure the guy understood everything he said. He wasn't sure he would have either, considering how the words came chopping from his shivering mouth.

They ran forward as fast as their stiff frames would take them. Tony's pants had frozen solid in the frigid air, making it harder to move.

Shortly they reached the driveway. The truck's tracks were covered by those with studded radials, and even those were filling in quickly with fresh snowfall.

In a minute the two of them reached a car. A white Pontiac Bonneville with two sets of footprints leading up the driveway. Damn!

"Just a minute," Tony said, pulling Frank to a halt. He pulled out his flashlight to check the license plates and then shone the light around to both sides of the car. It might work, he thought. "You know whose car that is?" Tony asked Frank.

He gave Tony his stupid look again and he knew the answer to that question. Tony pulled out a jackknife and slit a couple of tires, knowing they'd have maybe one spare. It would slow them down.

Without saying anything else, they ran off to Tony's truck.

Rattling keys to get in, Tony finally got his door open and reached across to open the passenger door for Frank.

Without warning, Panzer growled and lunged toward Frank Peroni as he was getting in.

Jumping backward, Frank yelled, "What the fuck is that?"

"Panzer. Behind the seat."

The dog turned and jumped behind the front seats.

"Get in! It's just my dog."

Reluctantly, Peroni did what Tony said, his head turned to buckle up and his eyes watching the dog.

"Damn thing looks like a bear."

In the truck now, the engine warming, Tony cranked up the heat. Before getting in, he had seen a place to back around. And since the truck had four-wheel-drive, he had no problem backing into the trees and turning around.

Slowly driving down the lane, Tony came to a stop out front of the Bonneville. Then he turned to the left and plowed through some small pines, angled around, and came back on the road behind the car. A few seconds later they were out on the main road, the heater blowing full blast, and Tony trying to keep the vehicle on the slippery road with numb fingers.

It took them more than an hour to get back to the condo, park the truck in the garage, strip down to their shorts, and soak their bodies in the hot tub. Tony had pulled out a couple of beers and they were enjoying those.

"What the hell just happened?" Frank asked.

"That's a good question. I wish I had a good answer." He hesitated. "You were going to tell me about the guys in the Bonneville."

Frank shook his head and took a sip of beer. "What do you want from me?"

"Let's start with the truth," Tony said. "Just before we were rudely interrupted, you were going to tell me what happened after you and Barb Humphrey got it on the night she died."

"Oh, yeah. That. Well, we're right in the place to tell the story. I was in the Humphrey hot tub suckin' down some suds, waiting for Barb to join me, when all hell broke loose." He thought for a moment, trying to remember the night, or maybe trying to forget.

"Go on."

"I heard a shot. At first I didn't know what it was. You don't think a shot is a shot; not coming from a nice place like that."

"The Humphrey place."

He nodded. "Yeah. I had left the back sliding glass door ajar, so the shot seemed to echo back out onto the patio toward me. I was ready to get out, but I froze. I'm not a coward, I'll tell you that right now. But I don't like guns. A gun is the great equalizer of all time. You could be some scrawny fuck and take out a huge football player with a single shot. Now that's power in the wrong hands."

"Back to the story. What happened next? You froze. Then what?"

"Hey, fuck you!"

"I didn't mean it that way. Go ahead."

"I heard a second shot and then someone came running out the door. Fairly tall. Fairly gangly. That's all I could tell in the darkness."

"You didn't see who it was?"

"Like I said, it was dark. And I'd had a few beers."

"But it was a man. You're sure of that."

"I think I can tell a man from a woman." He took a long drink of beer. "This is good shit. You got any more?"

Tony reluctantly got out and went dripping and sloshing to the kitchen for two more beers. When he came back, Frank was leaning back, his arms spread out along the sides, and his eyes closed.

Climbing back into the hot tub, Tony said, "Make yourself at home."

Frank took a beer from Tony and smiled. "Hey, after getting shot at, racing down a snowy hill like a fuckin' maniac, and then nearly drowning in the river...not to mention almost freezing to death, this feels pretty damn good."

Tony had to agree with him. His problem was trying to understand why the two Portland cops would try to shoot them. Frank Peroni wasn't telling him the whole truth.

"What happened after the guy ran from the house?" Tony asked.

"The scene took a definite turn for the worse. The guy ran off through the woods, so I started to get out of the hot tub. Just then the place blew up. I'd never seen anything like it."

Frank went on and on explaining how the flames had billowed out of the house. How there wasn't a damn thing he could do about it. How he had panicked and run to his car, driving back to his condo naked. How he was lucky he had taken his pants out onto the patio with him, so he'd at least have his keys and wallet. Tony listened to the guy talk. Watched his facial expressions. And believed what Frank Peroni was saying. One more thing he knew as fact. He had been scared. Scared enough to hole up in the cabin for two weeks. But that still didn't explain the two cops who were after him. Shabato and Reese. Or why they would try to take him out.

When Frank was done talking, and done with the second beer, Tony got them both another and then they both toweled off and changed into sweats and T-shirts. They sat in the living room.

"There's something more than you're telling me, Frank."

He responded with a subdued turning down of his head.

"Tell me about your job with Cascade Lock, and those two guys who shot at us tonight."

"I don't know who they are," he said. "You gotta believe me."

He wasn't very convincing. "Well, I don't."

Frank thought things over for a minute, and finally said, "I think they're from Portland. After the Humphrey explosion, I took off back to my place. I get home and find this white Bonneville out front, two guys standing at the door talking with my wife."

"The next day?"

"Yeah. The next morning."

"They looked like cops, so I took off."

That was strange. Why would they have been there so soon? They had told him Frank was under investigation for a number of robberies in the area, but why come to his place then?

Frank continued. "I came back to Central Oregon, remembered my boss's place along the Metolius, and I've been there ever since."

"Your boss, Burton, brought you there a few times?" Tony asked.

"Yeah. He'd bring a bunch of us reps there in the fall during hunting season. Of course the only thing we'd hunt was pussy. We'd get trashed for a few days, make the rounds to Bend and Redmond pick-up joints, and then head home. Last time was October."

That was interesting. Tony wasn't a hundred percent sure the two cops hadn't followed him there somehow, his eyes concentrating on the snowy road, but it was more likely they had finally gotten the location from James Burton at Cascade Lock. If he could track down the guy with his limited resources, it wouldn't have been hard for the Portland cops to do the same thing. But the timing was what bothered him. It was too much of a coincidence to have the two cops and him show up at exactly the same time in a blizzard. No, the more and more he thought about it, they had somehow managed to follow him there. And that pissed off Tony.

CHAPTER 28

Tony had a hard time sleeping that night. Too much had happened and too many questions were still unanswered.

So when he got up just as the sun was doing the same thing, he was alone for a while drinking his coffee. He had almost forgotten he was planning on hopping a flight to San Francisco that day to talk with the software company that was making a bid for Deschutes Enterprises. He made a few phone calls. First he caught Captain Al Degaul at home, told him what had happened, and asked him if he could look into Shabato and Reese more thoroughly. Degaul reluctantly agreed, saying he'd get back with him later in the day. Next, he called the local sheriff and told him he had Frank Peroni with him, what had happened the night before, what he had told him about the night Dan and Barb had died, and asked him if the two Portland cops had talked with him yet. They hadn't. He told Tony to bring Frank by his office for questioning. Tony agreed.

When he got off the phone with Sheriff Green, he went to the sliding glass door overlooking the golf course. The snow that had fallen the night before glistened as the sun shone off it. If he had been smart, which he was beginning to question, he would have said the hell with it and gone up near Mount Bachelor snow shoeing in the back country. There had to be at least three feet of fresh powder up there, since there was a good foot and a half in Bend. Hell, he could just take a snow shoe trek across the golf course.

As he stood there thinking, he was surprised when there was a knock at the door.

Panzer jumped to his feet and ran to the door, his nose working overtime. Satisfied, the dog walked back to his pad near the fireplace and lay down.

"Some watch dog you are," Tony said. He went over and peered through the peep hole. Cliff Humphrey. Tony opened the door for him and let him in.

"I'm sorry to stop by so early," he said. He was wearing one of his fine suits again. Only his pack boots with his wool pants tucked into them looking strangely out of place.

"What can I do for you?"

His eyes turned quickly from Tony to the spare bedroom, as Frank Peroni appeared in his underwear. Make that Tony's underwear. When Frank saw Humphrey, he avoided eye contact and limped directly to the kitchen for a cup of coffee.

"Sorry," Humphrey said. "I didn't know you had company." He started for the door, but Tony grabbed his arm.

"You can stop the act, Frank," Tony said. "I know the two of you know each other."

Frank came back with a cup of coffee, sipping once before sitting in a leather chair, his leg over one arm like Tony had found him at the cabin the night before.

Humphrey glanced Tony's way, unsure what to say. "We barely know each other," he said. "Mr. Peroni won a few bids on our developments. That's it."

What else could there have been? Tony looked at Frank.

Frank shrugged and said, "Mr. Humphrey threw a few bucks my way."

"Did you know that Dan was his son?" Tony asked him.

"Not until we got to the house," Frank said. "I remembered checking the place out for its lock needs."

"What's this about?" Humphrey said, confused.

Reluctantly, Tony told him what Frank Peroni had said the night before, leaving out some of the more sordid details. When he was done, Cliff Humphrey looked shocked but also a little relieved.

"Then he didn't do it," Humphrey said, relieved. "I told you. I knew my boy couldn't kill anyone." Then Humphrey turned toward Frank Peroni, his expression changing quickly to anger. "Why the hell didn't you come forward?"

Tony stepped between the two of them.

"They were both dead," Frank said. "What was the point?"

"You little wimp," Humphrey spit out. "You let everyone in town think my boy killed his wife and then himself..."

Tony put his hand against Humphrey's chest, feeling something hard, like metal, on his left side. A gun? "Listen. He's here now. I'm bringing him to the sheriff to give a statement. Your son will be cleared." Tony wanted to say it, but thought better of himself for holding back. He wanted to say that he could now collect the insurance from both his son and his daughter-in-law. But he didn't. Instead, he said, "I just need to talk with the company that wanted to buy your son's software firm. I'll be leaving for San Francisco in a few hours."

Humphrey's expression changed. "That's why I'm here. The deal is going down today. The representatives from the company are in town, scheduled to meet with Larry Gibson at noon."

"How'd you find that out?" Tony asked him.

He smiled. "Like I told you. I have sources." With that, Humphrey headed toward the door, but turned and stopped before leaving. "This isn't over, Tony. I want you to find my son's killer. Will you stay on the case?"

What was he going to say, no? Besides, there were too many questions he needed answered. Some, he knew, might have had nothing to do with his son's death. But he still needed answers, nonetheless. He was curious that way.

Tony opened the door for Cliff Humphrey. "Yeah, I'll find the killer. I've been shot and shot at in the last few days. That tends to piss me off."

Humphrey smiled as Tony let him out. He probably already

knew that about Tony. Sources.

Tony dropped Frank Peroni off with the sheriff, escorting him into the office personally. The sheriff had been somewhat reticent. He was probably pissed off that his case, which he had already written off as complete, would now have to be reopened. Tony couldn't really blame the guy, considering that the physical evidence and witness memories would both be a little stale as time passed. But Tony had given Cliff Humphrey his word that he'd find the killer. A fact he had failed to mention to Sheriff Green.

After leaving the sheriff's office, Tony made tracks across town through a cluttered downtown toward Deschutes Enterprises. The going was slow. Bend got an average of twenty-five inches of snow a year, usually in piles of six inches or less. When there was more than a foot of the white stuff, the inadequate snow removal system had a rough time trying to find a place to put it. Consequently, most of the town waited a few days for mother nature to melt it. Now, the snow sat in banks right down the middle of the street. Only those with 4x4s were having any fun getting around.

Tony got to Deschutes Enterprises by eleven and sat in the parking lot scanning the place for rental cars for the San Francisco delegation. Nothing. He wasn't exactly sure what he wanted to do. Should he try to stop the deal? Or should he simply try to delay it until he could sort out everything?

Some things were starting to come together for him, but there were still nagging questions that wouldn't go away. Like why Shabato and Reese started shooting without so much as a simple discussion? And what did Don Sanders and his dead horse have to do with anything? Worst of all, perhaps, was a feeling in the pit of his stomach that told him his client, Cliff Humphrey, was trying to play him for a dupe.

Tony had some time to kill before the meeting, so he drove out to Don Sanders' place to ask him a few questions. The man was there and even a little more calm than the last time he had left him crying over his dead mare. Having only a couple of quick questions for him, Tony was there only a few minutes before driving back into town.

Before going to the meeting, he detoured by Three Sisters Realty. Melanie Chadwick was in her office and more than a little surprised to see him.

"Tony, what are you doing here?" she asked.

He closed the door behind him and paced a few times across her Berber carpet. He thought about the crunch under his feet when he had been out at the burned shell of Barb and Dan Humphrey's former house.

"Tell me something," Tony started, turning and looking her directly in the eye. "Why were you checking up on me for Cliff Humphrey?"

She had risen from her chair when Tony entered, and now she sunk back into it, looking much like a young child sitting in her father's chair. "I don't understand the question."

Shaking his head, Tony tried to make it more clear for her. "Why were you looking into me?"

She shrugged. "Cliff and I go way back. He's sent a lot of business my way. When your old Navy friend said you were coming, Cliff asked me if I'd check into your background. He leaves nothing to chance."

"Did he tell you to fuck me?"

She said nothing.

"There's plenty more back-scratching to come," Tony yelled at her.

She seemed confused by his anger. "What's your problem? That's the way business is done."

"You have a lot to gain from that destination resort."

"So."

"So, maybe you had too much to gain."

"What's that supposed to mean?"

"You and Cliff had a deal going there. First, you sell him the land, making a nice commission. Then you broker an exclusive deal to sell lots at his resort, and probably even the homes themselves."

She let out a deep breath and seemed to sink farther into the chair. "You just summed up the nature of my business. So what?"

Tony thought for a minute. She was right. So what? What did it all mean? It wasn't likely that she had had anything to do with trying to break the back of Don Sanders by having his place wiped out and his mare killed. And did any of this have anything to do with the murder of Dan and Barb? He had no evidence to support that. Without saying another word, he drifted toward the door.

"You think I had something to do with Dan and Barb?" she yelled at him.

Tony heard the chair slam back and Melanie rushing toward him. When he turned, it was just in time to block her flailing arms striking at his head as she screamed obscenities at him. He finally caught both arms, but failed to deflect her right knee coming up sharply into his groin. The impact was enough to put him on his knees and let go of her hands. It felt like his balls were up in his throat fighting for position with his Adam's apple. Somehow he expected her to realize she had made an error and start consoling him. What he didn't expect was the business end of the sharp toe of her cowboy boots. After the third or fourth kick to the ribs, he finally managed to catch her foot and flip her to her butt.

Tony rolled over and landed right between her legs and then shuffled his body onto hers and pinned her to the carpet. It took every once of power to hold her still.

The door swung open and the secretary poked her head around to see what all the racket was about. Melanie and Tony both turned to look at her.

"Oh," the secretary said. "It sounded like something else." She closed the door behind her.

Melanie started laughing and her arms and legs loosened up.

Tony rolled over and tried to rearrange the boys, unsure if laughter was the appropriate thing at this point.

"She actually thought this was rough sex," she said, and then laughed even louder.

Tony sat up, still holding his nuts.

"I'm sorry," she said. "I know it's not funny. It's just...funny." She laughed again.

Tony was starting to look for a camera, thinking he might end up on one of those blooper shows Frank Peroni's wife liked so much. Maybe even win some money. He made it to his feet and she reached her arms up. The expression on her face confused him. Embarrassed indifference. Or was it disgusted repugnance? Nonetheless, he helped her to her feet and they stared at each other for a moment, unsure how to heal the situation. And, at least on Tony's part, uncertain if it was worth the effort.

Finally, he said, "Do you know what it's like when someone does that to you? Of course you don't. How could you?"

"My ex tried to explain it to me a few times." She smiled.

"A few times? And you divorced him?"

"Yeah, it's a strange world we live in, Tony. I hope I didn't do any permanent damage."

Tony went for the door again, grabbed the handle, and noticed something one more time. The lock. It was a Cascade. She was right behind him, her hand on his shoulder.

"I'm sorry, Tony. I really am. Can we still be friends?" She snuggled against his shoulder. "Or more than that?"

This woman was psycho. First she knees his homeboys, and then she wants to put the master of the house back in action. He shook his head as he opened the door.

"Let me think about it," Tony said. He knew it was a lame thing to say. On reflection, he had probably said a lot of lame things to women who he had no intention of seeing again. It's a curse that he would have to take with him to the grave.

Closing the door behind him, Tony got the hell out of there as fast as he could, trying his best to keep his balls from bashing against his legs. He thought he heard the canned laughter of feminism wafting up from the den of estrogen behind him. Maybe his one good ear was playing tricks on him. He drove off toward the meeting, thinking at the time that not much worse could go wrong for the day.

CHAPTER 29

There he sat again in front of Deschutes Enterprises. A few cars in the lot screamed of rental. Checking his watch, he saw it was closing in on noon. Tony got out and made his way up the slippery walk, still trying to recover from the groin shot from Melanie.

The receptionist, Susie, met him with a smile as he entered. The nose ring was gone, Tony noticed. Perhaps that wasn't the image Larry Gibson wanted to impress on the new buyers from San Francisco.

"How are you, Mr. Caruso?" Susie asked.

"Been better." He glanced toward Larry Gibson's office. The door was open, but from what he could tell the place was empty. "Is Mr. Gibson in?"

She shuffled some papers on her desk, trying her best not to look at him. "I'm sorry," she finally said. "He's in a meeting."

"I know that. I just need to know where. The conference room. I'll bet that's right down this way." Tony moved around her desk toward a room with windows to the floor. There were curtains closed, but he guessed that's where the show was, since he could hear voices as he got closer. Susie caught up to him and grabbed his jacket.

"Please, Mr. Caruso," she pleaded. "I'll lose my job."

Tony stopped and faced her. "Are you innocent in all this?"

"What do you mean?"

"Why'd you give the Blazers tickets to Don Sanders?"

Her eyes rose sharply and Tony had his answer. She was speechless, so he left her there with a stupid look on her face and barged into the conference room.

Tony was sure there must have been a better way to confront the situation. Especially after he saw the looks on the faces of those in their nice suits, gathered around the oval oak table. Larry Gibson looked like a middle linebacker on PCP, his eyes the size of walnuts. The three from the Bay Area looked confused.

"What in the hell are you doing here, Caruso?" Gibson forced out. He looked beyond Tony at his perplexed receptionist. "I told you no interruptions."

"I'm sorry," she said. "But he's a little bigger than me." With that, she closed Tony into the room as she slammed the door.

One of the three men from San Francisco turned to Gibson. "What's this about?"

"Do I need to call the sheriff, Caruso?"

"Please do." Tony directed his gaze on the apparent leader of the San Francisco contingent. It all came to him in a rush. "Sir, I'd like you to know that any deal signed today will be stuck in probate for years."

"What?" the man cast his eyes on Gibson. "What's he talking about?"

"He doesn't know what he's talking about," Gibson said. "That's obvious." He picked up the phone and thought for a moment.

"You could call nine, one, one, if you think this is an emergency," Tony said.

"You told me the company was yours, free and clear," the man from San Francisco said.

"It is," Gibson said, glaring at the phone, unsure what to do.

"You forgot about Cliff Humphrey," Tony reminded him. "He's the direct beneficiary of Dan, and therefore has claim to his property. In other words, you have a new partner Larry."

Gibson had this incredulous look on his face, as if he had just found a cockroach in his soup. The men from San Francisco didn't waste time or words. They simply gathered all of their papers into their briefcases, slammed them shut, and got up to leave.

"Call us when you get this squared away," the leader of the group said just before trudging out through the door after his colleagues.

"But wait," Gibson said, trying to follow after them. But it was too late. They were gone. When he realized this, he turned back toward Tony. "What in the fuck have you just done to me?"

Tony pushed his way past him, shoving him against the door, and then stopped and turned. "You should have read that partnership deal a little more closely," Tony said. "Have a nice day." He left Gibson there, his face red and puckered like he'd just swallowed a jar of hot peppers.

"You fucker," he yelled after Tony. "You fucking bastard. This isn't over."

As Tony passed Susie, he said to her, "You might want to consider a new job."

By the time Tony reached the parking lot, the California contingent was already gone. He got into the truck and sat for a moment, wondering if he had just done the right thing. Strangely enough, his thoughts drifted to Dawn Sanders. Maybe it was the new bruises from Melanie's boots kicking his ribs. Maybe he needed someone who was more pure, or at least open. Someone without an agenda.

Before he left, he called the sheriff on his cell phone. It took a while before he came on the line, and he was huffing and puffing with the effort.

"Yeah," Sheriff Green said.

"What the hell happened to you?" Tony asked. "Just finish a marathon."

"Fuck you! What the hell you want? And thanks a helluva lot, by the way."

"What?"

"Now I gotta open this case again."

"You mean for the first time."

"You got anything constructive for me? I been going around and around with Frank Peroni. He's more scared than he should be. I think he knows more than he's telling me."

Tony thought for a minute as he watched the front door to Deschutes Enterprises open and the receptionist stomp out, throwing her coat on as she made her way down the snowy sidewalk.

"Listen, sheriff. Can I get back with you? I gotta talk with someone right now."

"As opposed to nobody?" the sheriff said, letting out a deep breath.

"No. Hey, check into Peroni's involvement with those B and Es. I'll bet he was the set-up man on those."

"What the...you think I work for you?"

Tony couldn't hear the rest of his yelling, because he had already hit the End button and shoved the phone into his pocket on his way out the truck door. Tony caught Susie just before she opened her door.

"You leave me alone," she said, trying to get her key into the door of her Ford Focus.

"I'm sorry," Tony pleaded. "He didn't fire you, did he?"

She gave him a half-serious look as she shook her head. "I quit!"

"Good for you."

"Yeah, it's just great. When I can't pay the rent, then what?" She slowly turned toward him, her mind reeling and uncertain. "Never mind. It's not your problem."

"I can help you find another job."

"Don't bother. It was a piece of shit job anyway." By now the key found its spot and she had the door open. She slid in, closed the door and then rolled the window down. "I want you to know I had nothing to do with Don Sanders."

Tony had started back to the truck, but returned with that revelation.

She continued, "I gave him the tickets to the Blazers game, that's it."

"Did anyone tell you to?"

"I think you already know the answer to that." She started her car and drove off, the tires spinning and throwing up snow.

Climbing back into the truck, Tony headed out after her. As he drove toward downtown Bend, a lot of questions popped into his mind. Questions he didn't have answers to. He had just blown a deal for Larry Gibson, yet he didn't know why. He had a feeling the deal was somehow involved with the death of Barb and Dan, and that too was unclear in his mind. And there were questions about Cliff Humphrey, Frank Peroni and the Portland cops, Shabato and Reese, that wouldn't go away. There was one bright side to all of this. At least his nuts seemed to be recovering.

When he got to Dawn Sanders' Naturopathic Clinic, he was told by her receptionist to have a seat, since Dawn was with someone right now. He took the time to pretend he was looking through a year old travel magazine, while he cleared his mind on this case.

About fifteen minutes later the back door opened, and Dawn Sanders led an octogenarian Chinese man out from the back. When he had left through the outer door, she came over to Tony and greeted him with a hug.

"What are you doing here?" she said. "Never mind." She checked her watch and told her receptionist she'd be back in a few minutes. Then she hauled him through a back corridor and upstairs to her living area. There was one bedroom upstairs, with a bathroom, kitchen and dining area. She led him to the living room, which was an extension of the dining area. The room was decorated in what could only be described as new age Chic. There was a painting that must have been Nepal. Tropical plants were spread about everywhere and rose to the ceiling.

"Nice place," Tony said, as he sat down on a round wicker chair that seemed to scoop him up like a giant hand. She sat on an oriental rug at his feet and crossed her legs.

Seconds later, he was startled when a six foot black boa constrictor slithered out from under the sofa and wrapped itself around her arm.

"Don't worry," she said. "Tzu won't hurt you."

"It's a girl?"

"No. Tzu. T.Z.U."

"Short for Lao-tzu," Tony said. "Author of the Tao Te Ching?"

Her brows rose. "Impressive, Tony."

What could he say? He had actually studied the philosophy while stationed in Asia.

"Does he make you nervous? I could put him away."

Tony didn't want to bring it up to her, but there was something very sensual about a woman and a snake. "No, that's all right. I just wanted to stop by and see if you might like to come by the condo tonight. I could make some pasta."

She smiled at him. "This doesn't have anything to do with your fight with Melanie this morning."

"What the...how did you find out about that? And no. It was all her. I think she has something seriously wrong with her."

"She falls for people too easily," she said. "But in your case I can understand the attraction."

Tony gazed at her for a moment, not knowing what to say.

"I saw a few of your photos today," she said. "At the gallery. Not many people have impressed me with Black and White like you. The lighting is exquisite."

Now he was embarrassed. This was his first showing of anything he had ever shot, and he was not looking forward to it. Photography was so personal with him, it was almost like sex. Something to be savored but not talked about. Which is why he had chosen Bend for his coming out party. He figured he wouldn't know anyone there. It was easier that way. But now.

Tony simply said, "Thanks."

They were interrupted by Tony's cell phone. At first he tried to ignore it, but he thought it was disturbing the snake, so he decided to take the call.

She smiled and stroked the back of the snake's head.

When Tony answered the phone, he expected to hear Melanie's voice, saying she was sorry she tried to crush his balls. But it was Cliff Humphrey. He talked; Tony listened. There was no question that Humphrey was upset. After he finished ranting, he asked to see Tony as soon as possible. He checked his watch. It was just after one p.m. Tony told him to come by the condo at three.

Ending the call with Cliff Humphrey, Tony shoved the phone back into his pocket and glanced about the room. He was hesitating for a reason. Sure he had come to see Dawn because he thought they should do dinner together, but he also had to talk with her about her friend, Barb. And he could sense that she knew something else was up with him. To keep her from having to ask, he decided to go the direct route.

"I've gotta talk with you about something," Tony started. It came out all wrong, sounding like he was about to break up with her, even though the two of them were not even dating.

"I know. It's about Barb."

"Jesus. Is there anything you don't know?"

"I'll admit I don't know much about Jesus." She grinned and then gave her serpent more affection.

"About Barb," Tony said. "I found out she was murdered, as suspected. But her husband didn't do it."

She looked up. "I didn't think Dan could kill her. But who?"

What must have been going through her mind was probably a series of thoughts. On one hand, it had been a nice little package. Husband kills wife, then himself. Case solved, no concern for the general public. Now, there was a killer running loose in a quaint little tourist town in Central Oregon. Disturbing indeed. It threw an entirely new twist on one's safety and level of security. Could it happen to her?

Tony didn't answer her question because he wasn't one hundred percent sure about that himself. But he had a feeling, much like Dawn seemed to always have, that the answer to that question would come to him soon. He only had a few more things to tie up, and he'd need his computer and a little luck to make that happen.

"I've got a few ideas. What I don't have is proof. You're sure that Barb was not having an affair beyond the pick-ups she and Dan were involved in?"

"About as sure as one can get," she said. "I think Barb would have told me, though. She had few secrets from me. She'd tell me size and position of almost each adventure."

"What about Dan?"

She shook her head. "No way."

That's what he thought. "I should probably get going," Tony said as he got up from the chair and avoided stepping on the boa's tail.

She unraveled the snake from her arm and set it on the floor and then got up to walk him to the door. "What time tonight?" She was very close now, and she ran her fingers through the hair on his arm. If he had been insecure about these things, he would have thought she was stroking his arm like she had her snake.

"I've got a little work to do. But I want to do dinner early. Could you make it by six?"

"Sure."

She gave him another hug and he wrapped his arms around her. It was the first time he had touched her as he ran his fingers over her back. She was firm and taut, unlike some women he had touched, where the skin seemed to flow with his hands. They separated and he thought about kissing her, but didn't think the timing was right.

They walked out together, a prolonged departure. She led him to the door and said good-bye, saying she'd see him tonight. When they had first met, he had this feeling they would get to know each other. A feeling that Dawn Sanders would become one of those lifelong friends. If that was the case, then why was he having such a hard time saying goodbye for just a few hours until they met again? His emotions were all over the place. He needed to get control. Finish the task at hand.

CHAPTER 30

Tony thought long and hard as he drove back to the condo. The sun had made a slushy mess of the roads, so he took it easy, not that he was in any great hurry. He had to make a few phone calls, look up a few things on the net, and then piece this whole puzzle together. Then the meeting with Cliff Humphrey, the subject of which he had no clue, followed by dinner with Dawn. At least there was something to look forward to.

Parking the white truck in the garage, Tony let Panzer out of the back and the dog immediately ran back and forth through the parking lot. Then he loped onto the berm where someone had taken a shot at him, lifted his leg and relieved himself on a man-zanita bush, and then worked his way back toward Tony.

"You got one helluva nose, Panzer. Come on. Let's go inside. I've got a Milkbone for ya."

The schnauzer made a hasty run toward the outside door and waited for Tony.

Once inside, the dog's nose again worked overtime as the two of them went up the stairs toward the condo. As Tony shoved the key into the door, something strange happened. Something wasn't right. He could sense it. Sliding the door open a crack, he noticed the room was completely dark. Strange indeed. He always left the drapes open.

Panzer's ears stuck straight up and his nose twitched.

Tony eased his way inside and stopped in his tracks as the

lights clicked on.

Panzer growled but waited at Tony's side.

"About time you got your ass home," said Shabato as he made a move toward Tony from across the room. Sitting in a chair was a rather bruised Frank Peroni. Standing behind him was the other Portland cop, Reese, his droopy eyes adjusting to the new brightness.

Shabato patted Tony down for weapons.

"Hey, any closer and you have to buy me dinner."

"You're a funny guy, Tony," Shabato said, his task of feeling him up complete.

"Frank. You all right?"

Peroni shifted his head as he hunched his shoulders. Tony had a feeling he would have said something if his mouth hadn't been swollen.

Casting a critical gaze on the two cops as Tony made his way across the room to the refrigerator, he said, "I suppose you guys wiped out my beer supply?" Tony glanced inside the fridge, wasting time as he tried to figure out what in the hell was going on.

"We got a couple a questions for you." It was Reese this time.

Tony ran the items in the kitchen drawers through his mind. Knives on the right of the dishwasher. Big bastard of a butcher knife, if he remembered correctly. These guys weren't here for questions. There must have been some loose ends to clear up, and beating Frank until he gave up Tony's location was one of them. Followed closely by both of them ending up as coyote bait out on the high desert.

"Hopefully I can give you some answers," Tony said, moving back into the living room. He had a better idea than the knife. "Although I'm pretty much of an ignorant bastard when it comes to details. So you'll have to bear with me."

Frank mumbled something and Reese smacked him across the side of the head.

"What the hell was that for?" Frank whined as he rubbed his head.

"For being a dumb ass," Reese yelled at him.

"Listen," Tony said. "Let's stop right here. As of this moment, I don't know shit for shit. I'm working on the murder of Barb and Dan Humphrey. If you two super cops have something to do with that, then we can talk. Otherwise the three of you can just leave me alone. I sure as fuck don't need any more headaches."

Shabato flipped his red ponytail over his shoulder and took a step toward Tony. He stopped when Panzer growled and took a few steps in the cop's direction.

"You better control that beast," Shabato said. "What the hell is it a giant poodle?" He laughed.

The dog growled again.

"Now you've pissed him off," Tony said. "He's a Giant Schnauzer. A German-trained police dog. Being a cop, you should know that."

"Fuck you!"

Shabato was trying his best to be intimidating, but it was hard for Tony to take serious threat from a guy with a ponytail. Maybe the Highlander. Regardless, the cop still had a 9mm strapped to his right hip. The only consolation so far was his reluctance to pull it on Tony.

Shabato said, "Tell us about your case." His eyes were still focused on Tony's dog.

Tony shifted his eyes intentionally toward his thick briefcase leaning against the wall next to the sliding glass door. Reese took the bait. He shoved his foot into the hard aluminum case.

Tony took a step toward him, but was stopped by Shabato's outstretched hand.

"What the fuck you got in there?" Reese asked, looking at the case with great scrutiny.

"There's nothing in there," Tony said, trying to be as casual as possible.

Shabato went over to the case now. "What do you think's in there?" he asked his partner.

"Shit if I know," Reese said, playing with one of the latches.

"Maybe what we're looking for. Maybe the two of them are together on this."

Shabato glanced Tony's way. "Is that right, Caruso? You got what we want in here?"

"Only if you want my dirty skivvies." Tony made a move toward the two of them and Shabato finally drew his gun and pointed it directly at Tony's gut.

Now Panzer bared his teeth and stretched his broad chest toward the cop with the gun. "Panzer, *sitzen*." The dog did just that.

"Hold it right there," Shabato said, and then glanced back at his partner. "Open it up."

"No!" Tony yelled a little too dramatically. "Never mind. Go ahead."

Now Shabato looked confused. So did Reese, only in his case confusion required some sort of higher thought patterns that seemed to escape him. Perhaps his mother had dropped him one too many times on his head as a baby, Tony thought.

Reese's perplexed expression came out as, "Huh?"

"Don't you see, Reese," Shabato said, his gun waving haphazardly about. "He wants us to open the case. Why is that, Caruso?"

Tony shrugged. "Maybe my dirty underwear will knock you out."

"Yeah, right."

Shabato looked back at his partner and Tony took that as a sign to make his move, pulling his cell phone from inside his pocket.

"Something's in there. And it's not your damn jockeys." Shabato turned to see Tony with his cell phone flipped open and his finger next to a button.

"What's that?" Reese asked.

"It's his fuckin' cell phone you idiot," Shabato said, moving a step closer to Tony.

"Hold it there," Tony said. For some reason the man stopped. "Think about it, boys. Until a short while ago, what did I do for a living?"

Reese and Shabato looked at each other, unsure what to think. Shabato took a stab at the answer. "Crazy motherfuckin' bomb jock. What—"

"Think about it, Shabato. You're a smart guy. We gotta build 'em to understand them, and those who try to blow the shit out of perfectly good bodies."

Eyes shifted about the room. Uncertainty. That's all it could have been.

Shabato looked back at the box. "You're saying you got a bomb in there?"

"Damn, you are smart. And the phone is?"

The synaptic connections were starting to work overtime in Shabato's head, yet that was nothing compared to Reese, who was now moving a couple feet from the case.

"Fuckin' A," Frank said, rising up from the chair. "Motherfucker's got you by the short and curlies. He hits his fuckin' speed dial, the number sets off a switch in the god damn case, and the crazy bastard blows us all to hell."

Tony smiled as if to thank Frank for filling in the blanks. "That's about it. Although I could give you a long, drawn out schematic, with details of each device. But I'd hate to bore you with details in the last few minutes of your life."

"You're bluffin'," Shabato said. He wasn't a convincing liar. Tony could tell that he was just as scared as his partner, who was now across the room near the door. Like that would somehow spare him.

"Are you willing to take that chance?" Tony asked him.

Shabato thought it over, his gun down at his side. "Let's go, Frank." He pointed his 9mm at Frank now.

"He stays here," Tony yelled. "I need him as a witness for the local murder."

Reluctantly, Shabato holstered his gun and went to the door. He let his partner scurry through the door and then started out himself before stopping and pointing at Tony. "This isn't the end of this, pal. And I'm sending you a bill for those tires you slit. Crazy bastard," he mumbled under his breath as he left.

Tony went and locked the door behind them. When he turned around, Frank was up to his waist in the refrigerator.

"You want one of these?" he asked Tony, holding one of the microbrews over the top of the door.

"Yeah, what the hell."

Tony accepted a beer from him and shoved his phone back into his jacket and then threw the jacket onto the sofa.

"Hey, easy," Frank said.

"What?"

"The phone."

They both took seats. "You bought that?"

"Hey, you're the one who threw me into an ice-cold river in a pitch-black blizzard. Anything's possible." He took a drink of beer and then pointed a finger at Tony. Frank tried to clear his voice. "I think I'm catchin' a bit of a cold from that. Should I send my doctor's bill to you?" He hesitated and laughed under his breath. "What is in the case?"

"My camera equipment."

"That's what I thought."

"Sure. Is that a piss stain on your pants?"

Frank looked down at his crotch. "The beer's sweating. I set it on there."

"Sure. So, what did those two beat you for?"

"How do you know it wasn't your good friend the sheriff?"

Tony didn't even give that one a thought.

"Those two don't need a reason to beat someone," Frank said.

"You gonna tell me the story? Never mind." Tony laid out his version of what he thought the three of them had been up to, including Frank's considerable skill at either re-keying locks or saving the records of those potential robbery victims. When he was done, Frank sat dumbfounded across from Tony.

"Son of a bitch," he finally said. "How—"

"That's not important," Tony said. "But you've got something that's theirs; I'm guessing money laundered from some of your escapades, and they don't seem like the type to give up until they've got what they want. So, your hiding out at the cabin had a dual reason. You saw someone run out of the Humphrey house, but you had also decided to take a little extra from the robberies. Stop me when I make a mistake. You see these two at your Portland house and you bolt. But they weren't looking for a robber, they were looking for a double-crossing partner."

He sat there drinking Tony's beer and shaking his head.

"Where's the money?" Tony said.

"It's around. I'm not giving shit to those two."

"They will kill you, Frank. And then they'll blame the whole thing on you."

He mulled it over, his eyes shifting with various thoughts. Finally, he pointed a finger at Tony and said, "Not without the money. That's what drives them, man. The money."

"Eventually you'll give in," Tony assured him. "They'll wrap an electrode to your balls and start zapping you until your dick sinks so far up into your body you'll think you swallowed a hot-dog whole."

He shuddered with that. "Jesus Christ. Sounds like you know that from experience."

"You need to go to the sheriff and tell him everything. Say you'll testify against the cops. You could get off with a slap on the wrist, especially if you also give up the name or at least a decent description of the guy you saw running from the Humphrey house that night. You give Sheriff Green something to go on?"

He hesitated way too long as he finished his beer.

"Well?"

"I told you. I didn't get a good look."

"Then why'd you run and hide?"

"Think about it. He saw me. There's lights in the Jacuzzi. And, he could have gotten my license plate before he took off."

That's right. But there was something else bothering Tony about that whole mess. It was coming to him now in a hurry.

"You said the guy ran around the side of the house. Which side?"

Frank closed his eyes as he visualized that night. "The right side," he said.

"Toward the basketball player's house?"

"No. The other way."

"Did you hear a car take off?"

He was in deep thought again. "Don't think so. But it could have. The damn house blew all to hell. I was asshole and elbows around the other side of the house, trying my best to get the hell out of there."

"What about the sliding glass door? Did you have to unlock it when you came downstairs after your romp with Barb?"

Slipping back in his chair, he cocked his head to one side. "No. That's weird. I didn't think about it until you just brought it up. At the time I noticed the door was open wide enough for some-one to step through, but I figured either Barb or Dan must have left it that way. Yeah, that's what must have happened."

"What about the screen?"

"There was no screen." Frank got up and headed toward the kitchen with the empty beer. "You want another one?"

Tony got up and went after him. "No. And neither do you. I gotta get you somewhere safe."

"But—"

"Shut the fuck up. You're coming with me."

Tony hauled Frank down to the Deschutes County Sheriff's Office, handed him over to Sheriff Green, who listened to the story patiently, and then handed him over to some of his men to throw into a lock up.

When they were gone, the sheriff sat back in his chair and gazed at Tony seriously. "Something's up with you," the sheriff said. "You gonna let me in on the secret?"

"Quite the intuition on you," Tony said.

"Women have intuition. I got a gut feeling you aren't telling me everything."

"I'm still looking into a few things. Maybe that's what your gut is telling you."

"It's more than that. You're holding out on me."

Checking his watch, Tony saw it was a quarter to three. He got up and started to go. Humphrey would be waiting for him at the condo.

"Hold it," the sheriff yelled after Tony, as he got up from his chair and caught him at the door. "We got a murderer out there. You start poking your nose around and who knows what might happen. It's not a great leap from two murders to three. And besides, I'm now investigating this case."

"Sheriff. I didn't think you cared."

"Well. It's just more paperwork for my people. And it doesn't look good for the tourism."

"You're quite the Rotarian, sheriff." Tony opened the door and started to go but then stopped. "If you can get a hold of Shabato and Reese, I can handle myself. Besides, I think most of my work will be in front of a computer screen tonight. But, just in case, give me your cell number and I'll update you later."

The sheriff gave him the number.

"Call me," the sheriff screamed. It wasn't a request.

Tony left him standing there. It was wrong to underestimate a local sheriff like Green. Especially a former Marine.

CHAPTER 31

B y the time Tony got back to the condo, Cliff Humphrey's Mercedes was already parked in front of the garage door that still had a couple of bullet holes in it. The car also blocked Tony from parking inside. Humphrey was slumped in the driver's seat, staring straight ahead, his hands grasping the steering wheel like he was on a roller coaster. The engine was running, plumes of smoke billowing from the exhaust pipe.

Tony got out. "Hang here, Panzer," he said to his dog through the side window.

Then he rapped his knuckles on Humphrey's car window. He slowly swiveled his head toward Tony and then powered the window down.

Smiling at him, Tony said, "You stay out here and they'll find your frozen carcass in the morning." When Humphrey didn't respond, Tony continued. "What's up?"

"Why don't you get in," he said. "Let's go for a ride."

Tony thought about it for a second, knowing he needed to get onto the computer to look a few things up before Dawn came for dinner. Despite that, he got into the passenger side and let the heated leather seat envelop him.

Cliff Humphrey pulled out and made his way slowly down the snowy road. He didn't say anything for more than a mile.

"I thought it would make a difference," Humphrey finally said.

"What?"

"Finding out my son didn't kill his wife and then himself."

Now it made more sense. Guilt had been replaced by misunderstanding. "Why? Because now you realize someone must have really hated your son?"

He turned to glare at Tony way too long, considering the condition of the roads. When he turned back to his driving, he said, "You do everything to raise them right, make them good citizens, and then this happens. How can you still believe in God after that?"

"Without evil, how would we know good?"

The car circled through a roundabout and Humphrey turned right onto Century Drive, which eventually lead all the way to Mount Bachelor some eighteen miles up the mountain. Tony checked his watch from instinct and wondered where he planned on taking him.

"Larry Gibson called me this afternoon," Humphrey said. "Wanted to know what my plans were with his company." He placed extra emphasis on 'his.'

"What'd you tell him?"

"He said you went to see him and stopped the meeting, temporarily."

"Isn't that what you wanted? What do you mean, temporarily?"

Humphrey slowed the car and turned onto a small road that for some reason had actually been plowed. After a few blocks, he pulled over and left the engine running. Clouds still lingered in the air, making darkness seem ever closer.

"You said temporarily," Tony reminded him.

"Larry signed the deal this afternoon."

"What? What about your son's estate?"

"The partnership arrangement reverted all company assets to the remaining partner, upon the death of the other."

Tony's mind reeled now. He had made a major blunder by not getting his hands on that partnership agreement. How stupid. Turning toward Cliff Humphrey, Tony saw it for the first time. His jacket was open slightly and there under his left arm was the butt of a gun, probably a 9mm automatic, but he couldn't tell for sure. Tony thought about why he might bring him way out into the sticks to talk about this, and his instincts told him things that reason could only speculate on.

As he reached with his right hand inside his coat, Tony flinched slightly and almost went for the man's hand. He slid his hand out with an envelope, not a gun, and stared at it for a moment before extending it to Tony, who accepted it but didn't look inside.

"There's a thousand dollars and I paid your emergency room visit," he said. "Plus I'll have the garage door repaired or replaced for Joe. Also, I got you a week at that condo on the coast."

Now Tony was confused. He looked into the envelope at the hundred dollar bills, thought about what was going on, and then shook his head. "What about the case? Finding your son's killer?"

"The sheriff will find out who did it, now that the case is really open again."

Something wasn't right. Earlier that morning Cliff Humphrey was adamant about Tony staying on the case. What had changed his mind?

"Are you sure about this?" Tony looked at the money again, feeling more like he had just been paid to keep out of it, instead of for anything he had done.

Humphrey nodded his head and checked his watch. "I have to go."

Turning the car around, he headed back toward Tony's condo. Neither of them said a word the whole way back. He simply dropped Tony off, said he could use him as a reference, and dismissed him.

Tony stood in the gathering gloom of sunset and watched Humphrey drive away, feeling something like a male whore who had just been fucked royally.

When Tony got back inside the condo, Panzer at his side, he sat for a minute running the entire case through his thick skull. Either he was the dumbest motherfucker in Central Oregon, or he had just been kissed off. Maybe both. Humphrey should have never done that. It was true that he had hired Tony to prove his son had not killed his wife and then himself, and he had done that. But why stop now? What had changed?

Tony thought about all those things while he mixed up a crock pot of pasta sauce. Dawn Sanders would be over in a couple of hours, and he had a few more things to check on the computer.

By the time Dawn Sanders got to the condo, the entire place smelled of garlic and onion and olive oil. And in the background Vivaldi seeped from two Bose speakers.

Tony took her coat and hung it in the closet while he watched her. She was wearing loose slacks and a tight sweater that made him realize he had completely underestimated a couple of her assets.

"It smells so good in here," she said, taking a seat in the same leather chair that Frank Peroni had slumped in only hours ago.

Without asking, Tony poured each of them a glass of Chianti, which she accepted and instantly started to sip.

Taking a seat on the sofa across from her, Tony asked, "How are the roads?"

She smiled. "Starting to ice up. All that snow melting, the sun goes down, and then the remaining water freezes." She got up and took a seat next to him. "You know you didn't have to do all this for me."

Tony took a sip of wine. "All what?"

"The cooking. The music. The wine. If I wasn't the trusting type, I'd say you were trying to get me into bed."

Tony hesitated for a moment. Maybe too long. "I—"

"I'm just messing with you." She moved closer to him and set her glass of wine on the coffee table. "Although I am usually up for some antipasto."

She slipped her hand around the back of his neck and kissed him passionately on the lips, her tongue slipping in and out. Tony kissed her back, the whole time wondering what more she could do to him than Melanie Chadwick had. After all, Dawn had called her sedate.

Dinner would have to wait.

Tony was under some sort of spell, it seemed. She stood up in front of him, and in perfect sync with Vivaldi, she slipped her clothes off. Her hands caressed her naked form like two snakes wrapping themselves around her, the fingers of one hand finding a nipple while the other went inside her. Tony found it hard to concentrate on anything but her. He had to face it, it was just damn hard. He stood and released himself from his clothes, meeting her in the center of the room.

"I was wrong," she moaned.

"About what?"

She reached down and grasped his erection. "I didn't think it could get any bigger than before. I was wrong."

Tony caressed her breasts as the two of them drifted toward the floor. In a moment they meshed together as one, their energy moving in rhythm, her hips pushing up to take in everything. All thoughts slipped from Tony's mind, as they both lost themselves in the moment.

Later they soaked in the hot tub, relaxing after dinner, sipping an India Pale Ale. It was appropriate, since they had experimented with more than one chapter of the Kamasutra. Tony was so relaxed he almost forgot about Cliff Humphrey or Dan and Barb.

Dawn brought him back to reality. "My brother Don called me just before I came over here."

"Yeah? Has the mother ship arrived?"

"Very funny. Actually, he said he's giving up."

"What?"

She took a sip of beer and then said, "He's being practical. Earlier today the county approved the land use for Humphrey's resort. Donny has nothing left, Tony. He has a meeting to sign the papers tonight."

"It's funny Cliff Humphrey didn't mention any of this," Tony said.

"No, it's not Humphrey," she said. "His meeting is with Mrs. Ellison. At her place."

Now that was interesting. "Really? What time?"

"What time is it now?"

"Eight thirty."

"It's in a half hour out at Cascade Peaks. What's the matter, Tony?"

Tony started to get up out of the water, but she grabbed his hand. "What?"

She smiled up at him. "Where are you going?"

"Cascade Peaks?"

"Why?"

How could he explain it? She had certain feelings, now he had a feeling deep in the pit of his gut that something wasn't right. First, Larry Gibson sells his company, and now there was a final push for Don Sander's land. But why sign the papers at nine p.m. at Cascade Peaks? That's what wasn't adding up.

Sitting back into the tub, Tony explained to her how Humphrey had dismissed him, after telling him about his son's company being sold to the San Francisco firm. He told her about what he knew for sure and what he had a hunch about.

In the end, she shrugged her shoulders. "Let me come with you."

"No way." Tony pulled himself up out of the hot tub and toweled off. Then he hurried to get dressed, as she watched him curiously from the warm water.

"I don't understand," she said.

Tony wasn't sure how much she needed to know. "How much did they offer your brother for his land?"

She looked kind of embarrassed. "More than a million."

"More than a million?" he yelled.

"But that's prime land, Tony."

Now he was even more sure of himself, especially after what

he had learned on his computer before Dawn had arrived. He hurried and finished with his pants, shoved his shirt in, and then grabbed his jacket heading to the door. He stopped and looked at her.

"He's also working a deal to blow up some lava rock," she continued. "He can't work in this town without them. He said he got that idea from you."

She was beautiful in that hot tub. He had every right to say the hell with it, strip back down, and finish off the evening with a flourish. After all, the Kamasutra was an extensive manual.

"Will you wait here for me?" Tony asked.

She looked confused now as she sipped on the beer and then set the bottle on the edge of the hot tub. "You think Donny's in danger?"

"I don't know." It was as honest as he could get. He wasn't sure of much.

"That means you might be in danger. Don't go. I'll give Donny a call and tell him to hold off until the morning."

"Good idea." Tony pulled out his cell phone and handed it to her in the tub.

She punched in the number and waited. "No answer." She hit end and handed the phone back to him.

He went toward the door and stopped when she said, "Wait for me."

"No!" He ran his fingers through his wet hair. "Listen. I've had people trying to beat on me. I've been shot and shot at. You need to let me take care of this. Besides, I could use one of those patented massages when this is all over. Please stay here tonight."

She had risen from the tub and her nipples were as hard as obsidian. Now she lowered herself back into the warmth of the water.

"Save me a beer," Tony said. Panzer instinctively at his heels, Tony made sure the door was locked securely behind him and headed for his truck.

As he got outside, he realized a couple of things. The temperature had dropped considerably, making the sidewalk an ice rink, and thick, dark clouds had moved in, making it impossible to see more than a few feet in front of him. Through all that, his thoughts were somewhat blurred.

CHAPTER 32

Having hoped to get to Cascade Peaks before Don Sanders, Tony was disappointed by how slow he could actually drive on the ice without sliding down the embankment. He had seen a few cars in the ditch along the way, but none of the accidents looked serious so he wasn't compelled to stop.

He still had the pass card that Cliff Humphrey had given him, so he used that. There was a young man in the gatehouse that he had not seen before. He simply waved while he talked with someone on the phone.

He wound down through the narrow lanes, trying his best to keep the truck from fish-tailing. When he got to the burnt out Humphrey place on the fifth green, he pulled into the empty driveway and shut down the engine.

First he gazed at the basketball player's house. Jamal Banks was definitely home. Nearly every light in the house was on, and the structure seemed to be bursting with rap music. In contrast, Mrs. Ellison's house had perhaps one light on that he could tell from that angle.

As he started to get out, the door suddenly swung open, wrenching his hand from the grip and pulling him out onto the slippery driveway. He put his foot down but it went out from under him. Seconds after he hit the pavement, he was struck by the first billy club on his right jaw.

Tony was dazed but not out. He rolled to his side and into the snow alongside the driveway, figuring on better footing. If he could get up.

The next blow was to his gut, taking his wind away. Then there were two of them and Tony's first guess was the MENSA rent-a-cops. Somehow he took in some air and flailed his arms and legs until he was in some form of stance. His eyes, although blurred, had finally adjusted to the darkness and he could see the two of them better.

Panzer growled and then barked from the bed of the truck.

As one of them shuffled in the snow from behind, Tony thrust his right heel back and made contact on the attacker's right knee. Snap. The man twisted over to his side into the snow, screaming in pain.

Before the man in front could react, Tony planted a downward elbow into the injured man's skull, knocking him out. Then Tony spun around with a heel hook kick to the approaching man, catching him somewhere in the left arm. A lot lower than he had hoped. The guy smashed his stick one more time into Tony's ribs.

That was it. Tony took the guy out with a flurry of punches and a final knee to the groin and elbow to the jaw. He too went down.

Tony was exhausted. He tried to catch his breath while he searched inside his pocket for his penlight. After he swiveled it on, he scanned the two men. Shit! It wasn't the rent-a-cops. It was the Portland detectives, Shabato and Reese. What the hell were they doing there?

He didn't have time to find out. He hadn't noticed, but Panzer was going crazy in the back of his truck, running back and forth and finally settling his nose against the side window. Tony opened the back of his truck and stroked the side of his dog's head.

Panzer licked the side of his face and Tony closed the door again.

Tony took a couple of steps toward Mrs. Ellison's house.

"Hold it right there!"

Tony shifted his flashlight toward the voice, and now saw the two young guys who he had fought a couple times already. Goatee and Flattop.

"Get that outta my eyes," Flattop said.

Tony did just that, instead directing the light at their hands to see what kind of weapons they held. Just their sticks. That was a relief.

"Listen, guys. I'm here for a meeting with Mrs. Ellison." Tony trained his light on the two Portland cops still passed out in the snow bank. "You need to call in these two here. They just attacked me."

"Caruso, you are such a lying motherfucker," Goatee said. "We just saw you kick the shit outta them."

"Look at this," Tony yelled, pointing the light at his jaw, which was starting to swell up to near-goiter size. He picked up a stack of snow and set it against his jaw. "How the hell you think I got this?" His words came out garbled now.

They looked at each other. "We'll go to see Mrs. Ellison," Flattop said.

"Yeah, that's smart. In the meantime, those two freeze to death. And that'll be on both of your asses." Tony didn't have time for this shit. "Call it in." He strode off toward the Ellison house.

When he realized the two of them were right on his heels, he had no choice but to go to round three with the two of them. Luckily, he had a slight grade to his advantage. As he turned to confront them, something strange happened. Out of nowhere came a dark figure flying through the air, the huge body cutting down both men as they approached him. There was a jumble in the snow as Tony shot his light at the mesh of bodies. Then the largest of the three rose to his feet, a rent-a-cop in each of his large, black hands wrapped around each of their necks.

It was the security captain, Beaver Jackson.

"I've about had it with the two of you dumb asses," Beaver Jackson said.

The captain glanced Tony's way, and he tried not to shine the light in the man's eyes.

He said to Tony, "I take it you got some business with Mrs. Ellison?"

"I'd like to," Tony said.

The two underlings looked like a couple of kittens being held by the scruff of their necks.

"Trouble seems to follow you around, Caruso," Jackson said. "Like stink on shit."

Tony nodded. Like the man was telling him something he didn't already know.

Jackson continued. "Get going. I'll take care of these two...and those other two." He swished his head down the hill toward the two Portland cops.

Tony tried to catch his breath as he made his way toward the Ellison house. He pulled out his cell phone, dialed in a number, and waited. Nothing.

"Damn it, Green," he mumbled under his breath.

He returned the phone to his outer jacket pocket. Then he went for the house.

For some reason the motion light didn't come on this time, which was fine with him.

Making his way up the driveway, he noticed fresh tire tracks leading into the garage. There were also a set of human footprints that hesitated for a moment near his location before moving around the outside of the garage.

There were a couple of ways he could play this. Sneaky or straight. He decided, since Beaver Jackson would make sure the cops showed up sometime soon, he would be better off going to the front door.

He didn't even get a chance to knock when the door swung open. It was Mrs. James Ellison. She was wearing tight blue jeans and a sweater that could have been the skin on a Georgia peach.

"Mr. Caruso," she said, her hand against the door frame. "Are you causing trouble again?"

Tony stepped forward and started to open his mouth, but pain shot up into his brain from his swollen jaw.

"Come on in out of the cold," she said, finally letting her Southern accent flow.

Tony followed her into the living room, where a real fire was blazing, giving the entire area a warmth that only flames can bring. Then she left him there.

Sitting in a high-back leather chair, a brandy snifter in his right hand and a disgusted look on his face, was Larry Gibson.

"This is just fucking perfect, Caruso," Gibson said. "I'll have you know that your plan to stop the sale of my company...failed." He swirled some brandy and then gently sipped a little.

Tony moved farther into the room.

Mrs. Ellison returned with an ice pack, which she handed to Tony. "A doctor should look at that."

Gibson finished his brandy and replaced the glass with an automatic pistol. From that distance it looked like a .22 Ruger. Tony's shoulder seemed to ache once the gun appeared, easing the pain in his jaw somewhat.

"I think Mr. Caruso has more to worry about than a simple broken jaw," Gibson said, waiving the gun about in the air.

"Larry, put that away," she said. "That rug cost me two thousand dollars."

Racking his brain, Tony tried his best to cool the situation. But he hadn't really counted on Larry Gibson pulling a gun.

"You have insurance," Gibson said.

"That's not the point," she said, her hands on her hips. "I bought that myself in Istanbul." She said the name of that city like it was dog shit.

"Folks," Tony said. "I think on T.V. this is where the bad guys say how bad they were and how the good guys, that would be me, says how many fatal errors you have made. Who wants to start?"

"I'll give him this much," Mrs. Ellison said, "he's got balls."

Gibson shook his head. "We don't have time for this. Our guest should be arriving at any time. Or should I say intruder number two?"

"So that's how it goes," Tony said. "I'm just some common

thief now?"

"You dumb motherfucker," Gibson said. "You think you'll walk out of here?" He pulled out a cell phone with his free hand. "Speed dial, pal. And our friends show up."

"You mean Sigfried and Roy? They're out making snow angels. But thank you for implicating them. I wasn't entirely sure that they were on your payroll. Now I know."

Mrs. Ellison went over to the bar and poured herself a drink. She looked nervous.

"You don't know shit!" Gibson yelled.

"I know shit when I see it, and I'm looking at it, pal."

Gibson aimed the gun in Tony's direction, his hand shaking uncontrollably. "All right, asshole. You're such a big T.V. fan, you tell me the story."

Tony hesitated for a moment. Delayed actually. He wasn't sure if his jaw could take too much action. But, then again, maybe the movement would keep it from locking shut.

"Okay," Tony said. "This is simple. Two young men start a little software company, which grows rapidly. One is bored out of his mind and decides he'd rather dabble in real estate. So he looks for buyers. The second man doesn't want to sell the company. First man kills second man and second man's wife, and then blows the shit out of second man's house. Stop me when I get something wrong." Neither said a thing, although Mrs. Ellison was starting to look a little pale.

Tony forged ahead. "You," he said, pointing to Mrs. Ellison, "are right in the middle of this thing. Your friend Larry blows up the Humphrey joint and comes scurrying over here like a rat. His car is parked in your garage like it is now. By the way, it took me some digging to find out that the E in HGE Enterprises, which says it's Mr. James Ellison, was actually bogus. There was no James. Only a Jamie. That would be you." He pointed his finger directly at her. "Jamie Montgomery, formerly of Mobile, Alabama. By the way, you're still wanted down there for various indiscretions, none of which compare to murder."

"Okay," she said. "Fuck the rug. Now you can shoot him."

"Just a minute," Tony said. "The story isn't over."

Larry Gibson looked at her and then shrugged. "Go ahead."

Tony let out a breath, moved his jaw from side to side, and continued, hoping he wasn't totally wrong. "Of course the G in HGE is you, Larry. That took even more research, since you were a silent partner. You wanted to go into that new resort with Cliff Humphrey. You'd be a big dog in town, instead of a computer geek. A real player in this development boom town."

"How could I have set Dan's house to explode?" Gibson asked.

"I'm getting to that. You couldn't do it without first implicating someone, just in case the local cops didn't buy the murder suicide. So you set up poor, crazy Don Sanders to take the fall. Someone has just ripped him off, along with some explosive devices and wire. He's pissed enough to blow up the son of the man he thinks did him in and who wants his land. I even know how you had your receptionist, Susie, give Don Sanders those Blazers tickets so he'd be out of town. I also found out you worked for your father over in the Valley in the summer during college. His construction company, as you know, does its own blasting. You learned well. But what you didn't plan on was me. Of course, how could you know that Cliff Humphrey would hire a former weapons expert to investigate?"

As if on cue to the sound of his name, Cliff Humphrey came in from a back room, his pistol aimed at Larry Gibson.

Gibson shot first.

Humphrey followed with two shots.

By the time Tony grabbed the gun from Cliff Humphrey's hand, he was shaking and sobbing. He dropped to his knees and started to cry. It was probably the first time he had shown emotion since he found out his son had died. He looked defeated and disheveled, his pants ripped and wet and his hair sweaty and matted to his skull.

Mrs. Ellison ran to Larry Gibson, who was now bleeding onto her two thousand dollar rug. Tony reached the .22 Ruger Gibson had been holding before she could pick it up.

"You've got everything wrong," she screamed at Tony. "I had nothing to do with Larry's little game. I don't know what you're talking about."

"Save your breath," Tony said.

He pulled his cell phone from his pocket and hit re-dial. This time the sheriff answered. "Where the hell are you?"

The sheriff huffed on the other end. "I'm coming through the gate."

"How'd you find out?" Tony asked.

"Dawn Sanders called me," the sheriff said.

"Well what took ya?"

"The roads are slippery," the sheriff said.

"We'll need an ambulance."

"Gotcha." He relayed that through his radio and then said, "We ran across Cliff Humphrey's Mercedes in the ditch about a mile back."

That explained his appearance. He must have run the mile in his business suit, slipping and sliding on the ice.

"Yeah, he's here. He shot Larry Gibson. Self defense." Tony looked at the man's wounds. He had a bullet in his right shoulder and one had grazed his left mid-section. "But I think he'll live."

"Ambulance is on its way," the sheriff said. "They just patched through a call from Beaver Jackson. Mentioned something about those two crooked cops. You run them over with that rig of yours?"

"Shhhhh.... My cell phone is losing its signal." Tony clicked off his phone.

Tony went over to Cliff Humphrey and knelt alongside him. "You should have let me handle this."

He shook his head and caught his breath. "I found out why Larry wanted to sell his company so badly."

Tony waited and listened as Humphrey sobbed.

Humphrey continued. "The San Francisco company wants to expand their operation here, bringing in hundreds of high-paying jobs. The majority would buy housing at a discount at our new resort. I didn't know. I didn't know."

It didn't help that Tony knew this, but it gave the term 'company town' a whole new meaning.

Tony drifted away from Humphrey. Left him there in his pain as the sheriff's deputies shuffled through securing the area.

On the way back to his condo, Tony slowed the truck when he saw a man dragging himself alongside the road. He slid past the man and then pulled over. Tony almost didn't recognize him as he got out of the truck and stepped toward the guy.

Dressed in a suit and tie, no beard, was Don Sanders.

Glancing up from the ground, his face covered with fresh shaving cuts, Don said, "A little help here." He rolled to his butt. "Truck went off the road a ways back. Broke my leg."

Tony helped him up and into the back of the truck, laying him onto the bed, while Panzer whined next to him.

"You take care of him, Panzer."

Then Tony drove Don to the emergency room and dropped him off, before returning to the condo to see the other Dawn.

CHAPTER 33

By the time Tony got back to the condo, he didn't know what he'd find there. There was only one light on, a night light over the stove. He went to the refrigerator and reached for a beer. There was a note on the last India Pale Ale. It read: "I hope you're up for a few more chapters."

Tony laughed as he opened the bottle. Then he pulled out some more ice and set it against his jaw. The swelling had gone down, but he didn't want to look at it, even though he knew it was only bruised, not broken.

When he turned around, Dawn Sanders was standing in the gloom of the living room. She was wearing one of his sleeve-less T-shirts and nothing else. She stepped closer and quickened her pace when she saw his face.

"What happened?" she said.

"Had a little accident."

"That's not what I heard," she said. She took the ice from him and gently set it against a point he didn't even know hurt. Almost instantly the pain started to seep away.

"What did you hear?"

"That you kicked the crap out of some people again. I say we should go into business. Did you give them my card?"

"Right after I told them to have a nice day."

She laughed, jamming the ice into his bruise, which made him wince in pain.

Tony quickly told her his version of what had happened, mentioning her brother would need a ride back to his place from the hospital.

"It'll take them a while to cast his leg," she said, leading him back toward the bedroom. "Let's see if we can't move some of your blood around in your body from the top to about mid-section."

How in the hell could he ever complain about that?

It had been a long evening. Later, Tony and Dawn had gone to the hospital to pick up her brother. His leg would take a good six weeks to heal. But, crawling along the side of the slippery road, his broken leg dragging behind him, Don had made up his mind to hold onto his land. He had even thought about getting another horse. Maybe two.

In the morning, Dawn Sanders and Tony were sitting at the kitchen table drinking a cup of coffee. Tony checked his e-mail on his laptop. There was one message from a woman in Coos Bay who wanted to hire him to find her husband. He had been missing for a couple of days. He fired back a reply saying if he didn't show up in a few days, she could give him a call. He gave her his cell phone number and hit send.

"I suppose you'll be going soon," Dawn said.

"This? I don't think so. Husband just decides to vanish. Wife says they weren't fighting. The most stable guy in the world. Probably out drinking beer with Frank Peroni. Besides, I have my photos showing at the Cascade Gallery downtown in a couple of days. I can't disappoint my public. I think I'll stick around here for a while. I think we have a lot more to learn."

With that she came over to him and straddled his lap, wrapping her arms around his neck. She kissed him on the lips and then along the edge of his good jaw.

He knew it would be hard to leave Central Oregon.

CHAPTER 34

Ι t took a lot of explaining over the next few days to convince
  Sheriff Green that everything was as Tony said it was. The
two Portland detectives said he had ambushed them and tried
their worst to get out of the mess they were in. Green wasn't buying that. Especially after Captain Degaul had called from
Portland, saying the detectives had been under investigation by
internal affairs.

The two Einstein twins couldn't give each other up fast
enough. Seems they were both poking around Mrs. Ellison's
place, which was not difficult to understand. Same with Larry
Gibson. Mrs. Ellison had copped for a lawyer faster than a
Columbian drug lord. She had some hotshot from Atlanta on
speed dial. She could even get off.

Tony would end up testifying on Cliff Humphrey's behalf. He
had shot second, trying to protect Tony. That's his story and he
was sticking with it.

Now, standing in the Cascades Gallery in downtown Bend,
Tony sipped a glass of merlot as he watched people go from
photo to photo, their appreciation evident to him.

"They're beautiful, Tony," Dawn said, moving closer to him
and wrapping her arm around his waist.

"I think they're all your friends." Tony said. "You know everyone in town?"

"Lived here all my life."

Tony's cell phone rang. He considered turning it off, but instead he answered it.

"Tony Caruso," he said into the phone.

"The famous private dick?"

"Hey, Uncle Bruno. What's up?" Tony shrugged to Dawn.

"Your aunt is making canoli. Your favorite."

"Yes."

"Yes, what?"

"All ya had to say was canoli, Uncle Bruno. I'll come to Duluth."

"That's a good boy, Tony."

"Just a second." Tony held his hand over the phone and turned to Dawn. "You ever been to Minnesota in the winter?"

"No," Dawn said.

"How would you like a road trip? My aunt is the best Italian cook."

"I'd love to."

Tony returned to the phone. "Bruno. Is it all right if I bring a friend."

"That crazy black beast of yours?"

"Two friends," Tony said. "Panzer and a woman I met here in Bend."

There was silence on the other end. Finally, Bruno said, "Damn right, Tony. Your aunt will be so glad to hear that."

"Great. See ya in a few days."

Tony clicked off the phone and put his arm around Dawn. Together they watched the patrons of Bend admire the faces of the world.

10 06

Printed in the United States
59151LVS00002B/250-276